Cover Photography by Christopher Marona

ABOUT THE COVER PHOTOGRAPH

The cover photograph was taken by Christopher Marona, a professional photographer from Durango. He was at the Rooks Ranch shooting images for a book entitled "Colorado Cowboys."

The cowboy on the horse is Bill Rooks, our longtime friend and neighbor. I thank him for letting my wife, Conrad Nelson, and me buy enough of his ranch to have a ranch of our own. Every morning when I drive into town and come onto the county road past Bill's irrigation pond, then through his giant poplar trees and ranch buildings, then find the horses (Including Conrad's Tennessee Walker, which the ranch boards for her) and see the cattle on the irrigated pasture – wow!

Krieger

A Western Novel

by

Grant Heilman

FOREWORD

"Krieger" came into being about twenty five years ago, when I was bored after the publication of yet another book about agriculture, "Farm." I saw, in <u>Writer's Digest</u>, a competition for a western novel to be made into a film. I read every Louis L'Amour I hadn't yet read and started typing into my new computer. I never heard back if I won the competition, but I had a great time writing "Krieger." I stuck a carbon copy (no digital storage yet) into my files, and went on to other projects.

Then five years back, my wife, Conrad Nelson, and I had the good fortune to find a new secretary (and gardener, and computer fixer, and...) named Shelley. By way of introduction to what I did, I showed Shelley my published books, all of them photographic and about agriculture.

Shelley looked them over and asked whether I'd ever written a novel.

"Well, as a matter of fact, yes!" I answered and pulled the carbon of "Krieger" out of the drawer where it had languished for twenty five years. Shelley took it home and I forgot about it. At Christmas four years later, she brought it back all prepared for the new world of self publishing, and we selected Amazon as a publisher, and here it is.

It wouldn't have been done without the enthusiasm of Shelley and the cheering along the way by Conrad.

CHAPTER 1

Mostly it seems it takes about ten years to grow a boy into bein' a man. I did it somewhat faster. I started out as a wild, scared, skinny blond kid, runnin' away from my uncle, whose idea of helpin' me grow up was a hickory cane across my back. He inherited me when my folks got killed, and all that was too much for me, so I left Pennsylvania.

That was just a little more'n ten years ago, but I was feelin' pretty manly now, riding my dun gelding, Tempter, down through the aspen along Santos Creek toward the old trail that came north from Santa Fe. I was on my way back to San Badillo, and I thought I was a man, all right. It was pretty quick I found I was wrong, but just then I seemed to have the world where I wanted it.

Those ten years growin' up I'd spent doin' a lot of things. I crossed the prairies in a wagon train that was mostly folks bound for the Central City gold find. I ran cattle from the plains of Texas to most places, includin' that beautiful Montana grazin' country, where the grass is so tall you have to stand in the stirrups to find the cattle.

I stayed with the Cheyenne one winter. I was goin' to stay on. I was, that is, until Colonel Chivington and the Sand Creek massacre. Afterward, I tried to figure out which side in that mess behaved worse. I only knew that my friend, A-Ta-Khee, came back to where I was hid and told me to git, and I went. The two scalps that dangled from his belt were white. But I didn't know if Chivington's men were any better.

Lately, I'd been drawn into prospectin' for gold. I'd gotten known around the West for havin' the knack of findin' it. My saddlebags, burned with my K reverse K brand, ridin' behind my cattle on Tempter, said I'd had a mighty good summer. When I was comin' west, the men who were on their way to Central City in the wagon train I moved with were crazy with the gold fever. It never struck me like that.

One of them, Jeb Tarkington, he'd been a teacher back in Ohio, and he had some books on geology and minin'. I borrowed them from him, one by one, and by candle light when we were settled down, I'd read them. Not that there was much written there that helped when it got right down to sayin' "Here's the place to dig." No one's much help then.

But as Pete Chalmers, who had been a cow punchin' friend of mine, had said, I seemed to have the touch. I still believe that's about the way it works. You have it or you don't. I knew, at the least, that I'd had more'n ordinary luck at prospectin'. And thanks to Pete and some of my other friends, word of my luck spread through the Rockies. As I found out, that makes you a lot of friends. Some you can trust, and some you want to handle like you do a grizzly bear.

When I came down from the Ptarmigan Mine, I'd had it with minin'. I knew I'd get that desire again, only not for a while. I wasn't hooked, like those fellows in the wagon train on their way to Central City. But I agreed with Pete that I had the touch, and findin' gold does have its purposes. There was enough ore in those saddlebags to let me move along pretty much the way I'd decided I wanted.

One reason I'd figured I was a man was that I'd spent a lot of time up at the Ptarmigan thinkin' over what I wanted to do next, and what I wanted wouldn't have meant much to me say, two or three years back. First, I'd decided I wanted to be a farmer. Oh, not like back in Pennsylvania, or even in Illinois, but in some warm valley out here at the foot of a snow covered mountain. I wanted to build a cabin on a little rise where I could look out across the valley and see my fields growin' stuff. There would be a stream alongside the cabin – you can't grow things in these mountain valleys without water. Even I know that. And then there would be a woman to share it with. At that point my plan got pretty hazy, but she was there.

My dun horse is called Tempter because he tempts people. No one's ever actually stolen him except one drunk up in Wyoming, and when he woke up the next mornin', he sure wished he hadn't. If he'd o' been sober, I'd o' killed him, but as it was, he was only a mite tender about the face for a few days. Tempter's a big, rugged geldin'. They claim duns have a lot of stickin' with it, and Tempter fits that.

He does stand out, though, and so I called him Tempter when I bought him from the man in Kansas that raised him. When I got him, he was already broke, the man said. But it took a good many miles before me and the horse saw eye to eye more'n half the time.

Tempter, he wasn't very happy when I saddled him after I'd put the packs on Polly at the mine this mornin'. I threw the saddlebags on Tempter, and he rutched around a lot – but he couldn't do too awful much because he was in belly deep snow up there. He worked his troubles out pretty quick.

I made him push his way down through the snow, openin' a trail for poor Polly. She'd never have made it if she'd had to break trail for herself.

It wasn't that I hadn't wanted to stay at the mine a while longer. Things were goin' good up there. But when it finally cleared off last night and I could see the stars for the first time in three nights – stars up above timberline are somethin' different from what they are lower down – I figured I'd best get out while I could. These early winter storms are scary up that high, and I wanted no part of tryin' to make out in that cave all winter, unable to get back down through the snow.

Also, I figured I owed it to me to get out of there, especially when I swung those saddlebags onto Tempter and he danced like he did. The three months alone, workin' from light to dark, had got me a good stash. That little pouch in the bag along with the hard rock, that little pouch had at least a dozen nuggets bigger'n the tip of my finger. They were lost in the finer placer dust around them. The rest of the stuff in the saddlebags came from hard rock I'd dug outta the vein at the edge of the cave. That's hard work.

Back in July I'd loaded Polly with an arrastra, all broke down into pieces, and we carried it up to the cave from San Badillo, and after I crushed the rock through the arrastra, I hand sorted the pieces and only kept the very best. I was satisfied that I was into somethin' big, maybe a bigger mine than I'd ever imagined.

Santos Creek splashed its way down through the aspen grove. I could see the water was higher than mostly it is in the fall, because of the early snowfall up above. Ridin' along the stream down to pinon and juniper country, I turned north to catch the trail to the cutoff into San Badillo. There'd been rain down here when it was snowin' up above, but the mud had already dried to dust in this almost desert country.

Takin' off my wool vest, I tied it back of the saddle with my slicker. Tempter enjoyed it more down here, and he struck out pretty smart for San Badillo. He likely remembered the grass hay in the livery there.

Mostly, I tire of towns pretty fast. When I left San Badillo in July, I was lookin' forward to pinon smoke from my campfire, to the sound of the late snowmelt comin' off Ptarmigan Mountain, and countin' on the loneliness of the mine. But now it was reversed. I was tired of the hard work, and I wanted dusty streets, even if it was a town like San Badillo. I wanted a steak, a bath in the hotel tub. I wanted to hear cowboys talkin' in the bar, and maybe I wanted the warmth of a woman.

As Tempter worked his way from the pinon to the upper trail, I daydreamed in the sunlight and left the horse pretty much on his own. The trail was almost unused these days, since they'd built the Santa Fe wagon road a mile or so below us. The old trail would never have done for wagons, 'cause most places it's just horse width.

I was half asleep in the saddle when Tempter stopped. I nudged him with my heels, without even lookin' up. He stayed still. Somethin' inside me said I'd better wake up, and I raised my head and looked along the trail.

There was a heavyset, short coupled, dusty lookin' road horse, and settin' on him was, just like the horse, a heavyset, short coupled cowboy with a stubble of beard he'd not worked on very hard the past couple days. I knew that face from somewhere, but where?

"Welcome, Krieger! I figured you'd drift by here sometime this afternoon. In fact, we could hardly have worked the time better. That snow just had to bring you down."

The gun glinted in the man's hand, held close to his soft belly that was saggin' toward the pommel of the saddle.

"Just move slow now, Krieger, and we'll see nothin' happens. Keep your hands on those reins, don't go near that gun, and then get off the horse, easy like."

He had to be a man more used to takin' orders than to givin' them, but he talked pretty sure as he told me what he wanted me to do. And that gun, that gave him authority. There was no arguin' with him, least not for the moment. But I needed time, and I took it.

Where? Where had I known him? It was in a dark room somewhere...the bar in San Badillo this summer. After I'd bought up my supplies at Juan Hernandez' store, and had stopped for a drink. He was the man came up, said he was a friend of Pete Chalmers. A friend? No friend of Pete's would likely have a gun aimed at me.

"You're Krieger, ain't you?" he'd asked. I'd swung around slowly at the question. There was some sort of edge to the voice, but his thumbs were hooked into his vest, a long way from his gun – no trouble there.

"That's right," I answered him. "How do you know me?"

"Never met you before, but I seen that dun horse over to the assay office this afternoon, and down here in Mexican country there just ain't too many blond Americans. Pete Chalmers, when I worked for the Circle R, he talked about Kurt Krieger, the blond haired man with the touch for gold. Used to joke that if you was swimmin' in the middle of the ocean, you'd duck your head and come up with a handful of nuggets. I figured you had to be Krieger."

"Pete Chalmers?" I asked. "He's around here? You'd better have a drink with me and tell me where I can find him. Last I saw of him, I left him in Montana more'n a year back, after we brought a herd up from Amarillo."

The man wasn't someone I'd choose to drink with. Even there in the darkness of the bar I didn't much like his looks. But if he knew about Pete...I motioned to the bartender, and he put out the glasses and poured the whiskey.

"Name's Tinker Barclay," the cowboy said, "and my partner here's Ferret

Watson." I looked over to Watson and all I could see was trouble. I didn't know then, of course, how much trouble I was lookin' at, but I felt it right away. He was a thin, mean lookin' man, not very tall. All the while we talked his eyes kept movin' from one part of the bar to another, not often on me, as if he was expectin' someone to draw on him from out of the shadows. I never figured then what was botherin' him, but I wanted no part of Ferret Watson.

"Pete's managin' the Circle R," Barclay continued. "about seventy miles north o' here, on the west side of the Sangre de Cristos. I used to move cattle for him, over to the new ranches in the San Juans. I did until..." He paused and thought it over a minute, then looked over to Watson and laughed. "Well, I did for a while, anyhow. He talked a lot about you and Montana. You prospectin' down here?"

My thoughts caught up with me when I heard Barclay say "Krieger, you gonna get down off that horse or do I shoot you sittin' there?"

I had to stall a little longer, but I moved my head up so's Barclay at least knew I was listenin' to him.

"What do you want, Barclay?" I knew damned well what he was after, but I needed more time still.

"In those saddlebags, or back on that pack horse, Krieger, you got the cleanup from three months of work. You never brought nothin' to the assay office since July – I got friends there, and earlier you brought in a big strike. Now get the hell off that horse!"

It was risky, both for me and for Tempter, but Barclay riled me. I swung off the horse alright, but I nudged Tempter around crosswise and dropped to the ground behind his feet. The whole thing started to turn into a mess right then.

As I dropped down, I drew my Colt and pumped a shot at Barclay. I saw the fire from his gun as his horse reared, and he slid off backward and lay on the ground...never moved. I felt the slug from his gun tear into my right side, and the word he'd said "We..." tore into my mind the same time the slug hit me...more than one person. Damn it, where?

In spite of the pain in my side, I looked around. I thought I'd might get tangled up in Tempter's feet, but he backed off, careful like, and moseyed back down the trail. I was still lookin' around. The pain in my side hurt like hell, but I rolled over, up against the stone wall was at the side of the trail, thinkin' it might give me some protection.

The flash of a gun barrel caught my eye. It was along the top of a big log, fifty feet down the side of the trail. I'd not looked that far along before. That'd be Ferret Watson. I'd stupidly not counted on him.

I started to swing my Colt in that direction, but it never got there. I heard Watson's bullet hit the rock ahead of me, then it ripped across my skull. I remember a white fanfare of light, like fireworks I saw once in St. Louis, then it all was black. My body must have slumped to the ground, and my head was already runnin' blood. It was a mess, and I guess I wasn't as much of a man as I'd thought.

CHAPTER 2

When I was recoverin' in the sunny bedroom, taken care of by Maria Hernandez, I began to put together the pieces of that awful afternoon. There were little bits of bein' conscious, but mostly none of it came back to me. I did remember Ferret Watson comin' down the trail toward me. When that ricocheting bullet creased my skull, I must have lost my gun. Not that it would have done me any good anyhow, 'cause when I saw Watson, I was too far gone even to have moved.

Maybe that saved my life, for I remember him stoppin' by me, and nudging' me with his foot. I figured he thought I was dead, and I let it go at that. I wasn't even sure but what he was right.

Then after, there was somethin' about two youngsters who came and stood over me. I remember openin' my eyes and seein' them, and hearin' them jabberin' away in Spanish.

And then, finally, and God bless him, Juan Hernandez was bendin' over me. The wet cloth Juan was dabblin' at my temple brought me around. When I opened my eyes, he said, "Krieger, don't move. Just lie still. You've been shot up pretty bad...too bad to get you on a horse. Miguel is putting together a travois, and we're going to try to get you back to the ranch. The bleeding has almost stopped, and if we make it to the ranch, Maria will get you through."

There was somethin' about my arguin' that I could ride a horse, but hell, I didn't even have the strength to move my arms. I did remember when they tied me with a reata to the travois they'd fashioned, and the pain as I was dragged along the trail, and the blood runnin' down my side when the wound broke open again. But after that I guess I passed out, for it was almost two days before I woke up again.

When I came around in the bedroom in the house, it was Juan Hernandez who filled in some of the gaps. "Tina and Antonio were up on the mountain searching for the sheep which had strayed up there. They heard the shots and hid below the trail. Pretty soon a rider came past. They knew Ferret Watson from San Badillo, and it was him.

"After Watson came past, they left their horses and crept up to where the shots had come from. Tinker Barclay, he was already dead. When they came over to you, Krieger, you were still breathing. They galloped to the ranch and found me."

I understood. "But my horses?" I asked.

"They're in the corral. Tina and Antonio trailed them down."

I had to know the rest, but I was almost feared to ask. "My saddlebags? On Tempter?"

Juan, he saw things pretty straight. "You are alive, Krieger. For that you are lucky. Your saddle bags held your summer's gold? The children, when I asked them, said they had seen the saddlebags on the horse, behind Ferret Watson. That brand..."

"The K reverse K?" I said.

"They knew it. For that, Krieger, you are unlucky. But you are alive, remember that. There is more gold, there would be no more life, not here, anyhow!"

Well, 'course he was right. I saw that. But I hated to lose the summer's work. After awhile I drifted back to sleep though, and when I woke up again, the room was filled with sunlight, and there was a pinon fire in the adobe fireplace that stretched across the corner of the room. The fire crackled and filled the room with the smell of outdoors. I just lay there in the bed for a minute and was thankful for bein' taken care of.

Movin' my fingers over the bandage around my head, I located the tenderness. It hurt, but it seemed livable. I tried movin' my whole body, and wished I hadn't. There was a sharp pain down in my right side, and when I ran my fingers down there, I found a bandage coverin' it. If I didn't move much, I managed all right.

While I'd been growin' up, I'd never been a religious person. Oh, on the wagon train we stopped for Sundays and read from the Bible, but I mean I never really gave thought to God and all that. But now I quietly thanked God for Maria and Juan Hernandez.

It took me several days o' lyin' there before it came to me that carin' for the sick was the whole life of Maria Hernandez. Death came pretty easy in these villages up along the Rio Grande. The nearest doctor was more'n a hundred miles south, clear down in Santa Fe, and I figured most of the local idea of medicine was herbs and maybe even singin' songs out in a Hogan – I'd heard tell of that west of there, among the Navajos, and there was some of that back among the Plains Indians, too. I'd seen it.

But it was most toward the end of winter, when I'd been there several months, that I really began to understand Maria Hernandez. It took a lot of thinkin' on my part, but I finally decided that she was takin' care of people all the time, because God had made it so she couldn't have babies of her own, and carin' for the sick took the place o' that.

Turned out that's how Tina and Antonio both became her children. Tina's parents lived way up the mountains in an adobe hut, tendin' a skinny herd of goats. They died up there of cholera, and Tina'd been found in the cabin, both her parents dead. She was sick, too, and was starvin'. Neighbors brought her down to Maria.

Antonio, he walked with a limp even now, and he'd been crushed when a carreta, one of those big Mexican wagons, slipped off a wet springtime trail and rolled into the Rio Grande. Antonio got thrown free, but the wagon rolled over him. His folks got drowned.

These two, though, they were Maria's children now. After I got to know her, I swear if she'd been offered a hundred like Tina and Antonio she'd have managed to cure them all, and to care for them after. Maria was makin' her house into a real hospital and the local folks somehow thought of her as a sort of miracle worker. Where love and care made the difference, Maria's patients recovered, includin' me.

The Hernandez family lived well. Juan owned the store in San Badillo, and he was buyin' up land around their ranch. I'd read a little about these Spanish grant colonies down here. Back thirty years when this was still part of Mexico, the government had tried to get people to settle this wild country north of Taos. They set up these colonies, like Culebra, Guadelupe, and San Badillo. They gave folks the land, like homesteadin' was later in the United States.

But it wasn't easy, 'cause some of the colonies failed, and the settlers got pushed back to Taos or got killed off by the Indians. San Badillo, Juan told me, got abandoned once. But it was doin' well now. Juan was takin' his money from the store and buyin' up more land in the valley. I learned a lot about irrigatin' from him, 'cause that's what it all depended on – getting' water to the fields.

When it came down to it, I envied Juan Hernandez his land, his doin' things, his importance in San Badillo, his knowin' about farming, and I suppose I envied him a woman like Maria. But I was clear enough in my mind – if I worked at it, these things he had would come to me too. I was sure enough of myself that I knew I could manage all that.

It was maybe what I saw as their happiness that I envied most of all. My own bringin' up, before I left Pennsylvania, it didn't have much happiness in it, and most the time I did my best not to remember back then.

But there was one thing I gradually learned about Maria and Juan that seemed to bring sadness to them – in addition to their not havin' children was really their own. I first heard of Marguerita when I was well enough to sit out on the patio east of the cottonwood trees with Maria. Tina had galloped up the drive, back from the village.

"She rides beautiful," I said. "You must be proud of Tina."

"Of course," Maria answered. "But she rides well because she has learned from Marguerita. There never was such a rider as Marguerita."

"Who is she?" I asked her.

"She was..." Maria paused, and tears come into her eyes and she couldn't talk any more. "You must ask Juan," she said, and she ran into the house. That sure puzzled me.

But I took my time, for I knew I was into somethin' pretty important. Several days later Juan and I had ridden off to take a look at the pasture on the east side of the valley. I was up to getting' on a horse, provided I went easy. We'd got off and Juan was studyin' whether the grass was doin' well enough to move the sheep over from right around the ranch.

It was him brought up Marguerita. "You asked Maria about Marguerita,

Krieger, and you found she could not speak of her." Juan did not look up as he talked.

"It was just above here, where the trail goes across the mountains to the north, that she was stolen from...but you must know the whole story, so let me start when she was a baby – and you will see why it is hard for Maria. You must understand, though, that the story is not yet ended, and some day Marguerita will come back to us. You call it, in English, kidnapping, Krieger. Some day we will find those who kidnapped her, and she will return to us, and Maria will be completely happy."

We mounted up and walked our horses side by side, back across the fields toward the house. "The beginning was fifteen, maybe sixteen, years ago. Maria and I had already been married five years and God had seen fit not to bless us with children. We had ridden to Santa Fe, where there was a woman Maria had heard could sometimes help in these things. But after Maria met her, she decided the woman was ignorant, only tried to get money, could do nothing.

"Riding back north again, we came across a detachment of cavalry returning to Taos. I knew some of the soldiers, for they had been to San Badillo when we had trouble with the Indians once. Two of the soldiers had even stayed in our house. When they saw Maria, they asked for her help.

"They had been west of the trail, they said, chasing a band of Jicarilla Apaches that'd been annoying farmers. When they finally located the Indians, the Apaches had just attacked a tiny summer camp of Utes and destroyed the village. The soldiers killed many of the Apaches, but a few escaped west into the mountains, back toward their home country. Then the soldiers rode into the Ute camp and found terrible destruction. All people had been killed, Krieger. All, it turned out, but one. The one who remained alive was Marguerita, and the soldiers were bringing her back with them.

"She was tiny, just old enough to walk a little, and the soldiers had seen her move among the dead up there. Had they not found her, she would have died quickly, and had we not come across the soldiers,

Krieger, she would have been dead before they got to Taos. She was badly hurt. An Apache had tried to kill her, and his lance had gone right through her neck. Here..." Juan pointed to the front of his throat.

"The soldiers brought the child to Maria. She looked and saw quickly the child was dying because she could not get enough air through the tube that goes here." He pointed to his throat again.

"You know, Krieger, you've seen sheep with their throats ripped open by the coyotes...it was like that. Maria looked at her, saw the trouble was in the skin and the pieces of flesh that stopped the air. Marguerita was already turning blue. With a razor from one of the soldiers, Maria cut away the bad parts...Krieger, I couldn't watch, it was too terrible for me. The soldiers were holding the little girl, but she was too weak to move much anyway.

"Maria, she had never done anything like this before, but she could see the child could only live for minutes. The soldiers, they were astonished as they watched, and when she was done, Maria said to them "I think the girl will live, but I will take her and she will be ours, and I will see to it that she *does* live."

"So that is how we had our first child. Marguerita was a Ute, but we both loved her as if she was ours. We of Mexican origin, Krieger, we are many of us part Indian, and being Ute makes no difference. North of here it might not be true, for you do not look at Indians the same way."

Well, I knew what Juan meant about that, for mostly Americans thought of Indians only as savages. Me, because I'd been accepted by the Cheyennes for a while, I didn't see it quite like most people.

Juan went on. "Because of the damage to her throat, Marguerita could never talk, only a terrible sound she just quit making as she got older. But everything else Marguerita grew up to do, she was wonderful at. She learned to read and to write – we had a priest here then, Father Lopez, who liked her and made her come in to study. She understood not only Spanish, but much English. And when she was old enough to be around the store, she learned to understand Ute from Indians who bought from me. She could do figures better than even I can do.

"But mostly, being Indian, she loved the outdoors. When she was only eight or nine she managed the sheep alone. On a horse she was more beautiful than anyone. That's why Maria spoke up the other day when you mentioned Tina."

But I wanted to know more about what had become of her. "She was stolen – kidnapped, you said. Who stole her? How?"

"Three, almost four, years ago, she was becoming a young woman, Krieger, she had brought the sheep up here just above where the trail crosses. She had moved them many times with only a horse and a dog to help. She did not return home that night. We searched with torches, Miguel, some other villagers, and I. We found the sheep, but Marguerita and her horse were gone. We stayed all night, riding the canyons, shouting, but there was no sound in return. She could not have answered, but she could have made a noise somehow.

"After daybreak, we found the tracks. Two horses had come from the trail. They met the tracks of Marguerita's pinto, then all three went back down, her horse being led by one of the other riders. We followed the tracks for several miles. They turned west on an old Indian trail that is sometimes used. It goes north beyond Conejos, and from there you can ride into the San Juans, staying south of the river. We lost the trail in a windstorm."

I wasn't clear. "She didn't just ride away with them?"

"No, no, she was kidnapped! She would never have left her home, or the sheep. We have heard stories sometimes from men who had ridden through San Badillo, of having seen the Indian girl with the men. They are outlaws, Krieger, and they keep her hidden. Several times I've heard of where she might be, or where she was last seen, and have ridden to find her, but she's never been there. Maria will never really recover until we find Marguerita again. It's the saddest thing that has ever happened to us. I don't know, Krieger, whether now she will ever come back to San Badillo."

I figured maybe Juan was right, she would never be found. But that was before I got to plannin' what I would do.

The longer days of spring made me anxious to move on. I watched the peach trees in the Hernandez orchard as the buds swelled. I helped with the lambin', and the flocks went over to the new pasture. I had considered myself a man, and while I had been at the mine last summer, I had thought much about what I wanted to do. After the winter with Maria and Juan, I was even more sure I wanted a farm of my own, but there were new things now that I had to do first, and my side was better, at least well enough I could get started.

Earlier I had wondered how I could possibly repay Maria and Juan for their kindness. Money was all right, but they were hardly poor. But now I knew that I would find Marguerita for them! The Rocky Mountains seem endless, but the number of people who live in them isn't much. I discovered that, when I found out that almost everyone I came across had heard about how I found gold easier than most. I figured if I moved on, kept askin' questions, maybe learned a little here and there, went on to where I'd heard anythin' – well, I knew that sometime I'd find Marguerita for them and could bring her back home.

Not that it would be easy, but I was sure it wasn't impossible. If she was alive, and if she was still in the mountains, I would find her and return her to San Badillo.

But there was another search I had to make, too. Ferret Watson. He was a thief, he had taken my summer's work, and he had shot me. I would find him, and when I did I would kill him. When I was thinkin' of Marguerita and of Ferret Watson, I had no idea at all how the search for the two of them would become the same! And if it hadn't been for Slim Carruthers at the Circle R I might never have been able to find either of them.

CHAPTER 3

Before I set out lookin' for the girl, though, I needed to go back up to the Ptarmigan Mine. First of all, I was healthy enough now, but I wasn't ready to tackle anything very hard. At the mine I could work along as I needed to, and get stronger. Second, I needed money. The money I'd made from the work at the beginnin' of last summer I'd given to Juan and Maria for takin' care of me. They hadn't wanted it, but I believe in payin' my debts. Now, at the mine I could find enough gold to allow me to live while I searched for Marguerita.

And last, I wanted to get back up there because I had been too much around people. Part of the time I needed other people around, but part of the time I wanted only the sounds of aspen leaves movin', a stream splashin', and the whistle of the wind at timberline.

The snowline was movin' higher up the mountains and I felt it was time to leave. Polly was loaded with supplies I'd bought from Juan. I saddled Tempter and set out down the old trail, across the pinon and juniper, and up through the aspen grove.

As we was movin' upward, Tempter didn't like how the snow got deeper, but I clucked him on gently. In the valley it had been spring all right. Up here it was still bitter cold, and I was countin' on the protection I was gonna get from bein' up at the cave. A long dark cloud came in from the east as I watched on the way up, and I found that peculiar, though I'd never been in these mountains in the springtime.

As I rode into the flat basin below the mine, new snow was beginnin' to fall. Up toward the ridges above me, I could see the overhangin' cornices, and they looked like avalanche danger to me. Swirls of snow were blowin' off the mountains and I hunkered down in the saddle, and urged Tempter across the basin. I'd been figurin' to leave the horses in the corral I'd built last summer at the head of the canyon. But as I looked up at the walls on either side, the snow buildup scared me. There was maybe two or three feet of snow still on the ground in the canyon, but the winter's collection hangin' there on the ridges was bigger'n I liked it. If that came down in an avalanche, the horses would be buried or swept away. It made me uneasy, just ridin' through there.

So I got off Tempter quietly, and pulled my snowshoes from the pack on Polly's back, and started on up the slope to the cave, leadin' the horses. There was a flat spot up there alongside the cave, big enough to tether both horses, and I felt safer with them out of the valley.

Brushin' the snow off the entrance to the cave where the mine was, I unloaded the horses and moved my supplies in. When I'd left in a hurry last fall there was plenty of wood stacked so I built me a fire. It wasn't exactly warm, but I wouldn't freeze either.

Walkin' over to the edge of the cave, I looked up at the ridges above me. The snowflakes were scarcer now, and I could see how much snow was up there. It was plenty, and right across the top edge there was a big smooth cornice. The cave itself was no problem, 'cause it was protected by a hogback ridge that went almost straight up the mountain, but that cornice scared me, and with it there I knew it would be too dangerous to go down into the valley to work the stream, even if I could blast part of it free of ice.

Once in Montana I'd watched as Captain Murch, an old miner, brought down an avalanche with blastin' powder. I'd brought up a store of dynamite, and I couldn't see any danger in tryin' it out. I warmed it mighty careful, 'cause I knew it wasn't worth shucks frozen. Studyin' the overhang to the south of me, I figured about where the base of the snow buildup would be, wrapped four sticks o' dynamite with twine and attached the fuse good and solid.

Lightin' the fuse, I heaved the dynamite. It went up there in a big long arc, and it landed in the snow just right. I raced back to the other side of the cave and talked quiet to the horses, 'cause I knew that all hell might break loose. I was right. The first roar from up there made it seem like it was in a hurry to explode all right. The whole mountain shook, and Tempter, he didn't much take to that. Then there was a long rumble and the avalanche broke loose and slid down the slope west of the cave.   Snow got tossed everywhere as it went, and it took lots o' rocks along with it.

It looked like the whole valley was in a giant snowstorm. I'd never seen anythin' like this, not even that time in Montana. Everything along the way went with it. Down below, the avalanche covered the corral where the horses would have been. Then pretty soon the air cleared and I could see it all. There was an extra ten or twenty feet of snow piled on top of everything down there. But the danger was gone now, and I could get on with my plans.

It wasn't easy work in the mountains, and I got my muscles back. After a while it melted off enough I could rebuild the corral and move the horses down there.   And before the runoff built up too wild, I worked the stream. Down there I already knew the rich areas and the riffles, and though I didn't find so many big nuggets as I'd found before, there was color in most every pan. The hard rock in the cave was even richer.   Workin' last fall had only touched the edge of the ore vein.   There was no doubt now, I was into a really big find.

But by the end of June I was weary of the mine. There were other things I wanted to get on with, 'specially findin' Marguerita. She'd stayed in my thinkin' all the time I was workin' the mine. That strange girl, I wondered where I'd finally find her – if I ever did.

When I got back down the valley I stopped to see Maria and Juan. I told them I was goin' on north, but that I wanted to do somethin' for them. I wanted to give them the Ptarmigan Mine.

Juan laughed. "Krieger," he said, "You are crazy. You can't just give away a fortune like that. You found it, you worked it, it's yours."

He was right, I knew that, but I also figured if it was mine then I could give it away. "Take it," I said. "If you find enough gold, build a hospital so Maria can have room for her patients. I have enough money for now, and maybe what I have will make happiness for me, too."

We argued some, but Juan finally agreed that him, his brother Miguel, and me would all own the mine, and that Miguel would work it and we would share the profits. We went over to a notary in town and he wrote it up like that. I didn't really know then how rich that mine would make me later on, though I reckoned it held a good body of ore. But I wasn't much interested in gold right then.

The next mornin' I left for the Circle R. I wanted to see Pete Chalmers.

CHAPTER 4

That valley gets hot in the summer, but the cottonwoods that lined the west side of the road to the Circle R ranch buildings helped cool it off. I stopped part way along the road to let Tempter and Polly have their fill of water. Out in the field to the west I'd been watchin' two cowboys hazin' cows in the pasture, movin' them up to the north end. They must've seen my horses 'cause they left the cows, come across the pasture, and rode onto the trail up beyond where I was. I got Tempter and Polly movin' toward the cowboys.

One of them, an older fellow with lots of wrinkles from the sun, coiled his lariat as they waited for me to move up to them. They didn't seem either friendly or unfriendly, but it looked as if they had a job to do, identifyin' strangers on the Circle R land, and I understood all right I was trespassin'. So, when they asked questions, I figured they had a right to know the answers.

"Lookin' for work as a hand?" It was the older man.

"Nope," I said, "Just lookin' for an old friend's up here, I understand."

"Named?"

"Pete Chalmers. Hear he's head honcho on the Circle R."

They both relaxed a little. "Where'd you know Pete?" It was the younger one this time, a square shouldered honest lookin' cowboy, maybe 'bout my own age.

"Up in Montana mostly. We ran cattle there a couple of years back. Brought 'em up from Texas."

The cowboys still hadn't moved aside, but I understood they had to be satisfied with me and who I was. Then the older fellow smiled at me. "That horse named Tempter?"

"You bet!"

"Shucks," he said, "You're Krieger. I'm Slim Carruthers, this here's Bill Crawford. Pete and the missus are likely up to the house about now. We'll leave these cows and ride up there with you. Sorry we held you up with questions, but we're a mite touchy about strangers – we've been having' rustlin' troubles."

"Pete's married?"   I hadn't heard about that.

"Yep, about four months back. You'll find her a right nice lady."

When we stopped at a hitchin' rail in front of the house, Pete came out right away, shoutin' "Krieger!" It sure was good to see him again.

The cowboys took Tempter and Polly over to the corral, said they'd see to them. Pete and I went on in and met Jane. She was thin, but sturdy lookin', her brown hair done up in some sort of knot, and I could see right quick she was sure of herself. I liked women that was like that. She came up, shook my hand, and looked me over pretty careful.

"Krieger," she said finally, "From the stories Pete's told me about you, I thought you'd be eight feet tall and have gold nuggets hanging from the ends of your fingers."

Well, I blushed and didn't know exactly what to say. I'd never heard an English woman talk before, and it made me somehow feel like a young kid just come in from Indian country – in a way I guess that's what I was, at that.

Pete, he saw I was kinda uncomfortable. "Pay no attention to her accent," he laughed. "Jane's English, and I had to marry to get my job out here. The Circle R's owned by a group of rich Englishmen. Jane came out to see the American wilderness and caught me instead of a bear." He put his arm around her, and I could feel they got along pretty well, and I wondered what it was like to be like that – you know, in love, and married. I hoped I'd find out sometime before too long, but I didn't know how I was goin' to go about it.

After supper I rode with Pete and Jane out across the valley, where cattle were grazin' everywhere.

"Most of our cattle are still out here," Pete explained to me, "Workin' on the early grass that hasn't dried out yet. We'll get them up into the mountains before long, though we've got problems with rustlers and I don't know whether the mountains or these open fields are safer.

"This all belongs to the Circle R, just about as far as you can see. It was originally a Spanish grant, and when the owners ran into trouble, one of the English syndicate partners was in Denver looking for land, and they picked this up. Tom Morgan, you remember him from the ranch in Montana, he recommended me as boss, and here I am on a new job on a new ranch with a new wife, and Krieger, I could hardly be happier – except maybe for the rustling. We've got to get that under control somehow.

"Mostly, you can see the herd's top grade cattle, that's the kind rustlers like – might as well steal good ones as bad ones, I guess. We're plannin' to build up markets both east and west of here. East they go to market, so they get the culls, west we're selling breeding stock to the ranches that are starting up in the San Juans, and across Cochetopa into the Gunnison Valley."

"I ran across a couple of cowboys delivered cattle for you into the San Juans," I recalled.

"Who's that?" Pete asked.

"Fellows named Tinker Barclay, and a sidekick of his named Ferret Watson."

Well, it was pretty clear from Pete's expression those two weren't exactly favorites of his.

"Don't call those bastards cowboys of mine. They ran one bunch of cattle back to the mountains for me, lost half of them, or said they did. I found out later they ran them off and sold them down in New Mexico. They had the nerve to come back here, but I kicked them off the place. Should probably have shot them. Where'd you ever see them anyhow?"

"First time was in a bar in San Badillo. Next time they were on a trail east of there, waitin' for me. Barclay's dead, I had to kill him. But Ferret Watson, he's gone, along with my last summer's gold, and part of my hide. He's the one I want to find. He not only got my gold, he gave me this." I pulled my hair aside, showed the scar where Watson's bullet creased my skull. Pete and Jane seemed impressed, all right.

"You'll find him some day, Krieger. You know his brother, the one they call Trigger? He claims to be a gunfighter, but we think he's more a cattle rustler – so far, though we've not caught him at it."

Nothin' would do but that I stay on a few days. I rode the ranch with Pete, watched as he superintended the hands who were checkin' cattle, mendin' fence, shifting irrigation ditches – all the regular chores of a giant ranch like the Circle R. I guess maybe I was jealous sometimes, but Pete was a top man, and he deserved a spread like the Circle R.

He was edgy though, and I couldn't blame him. Those cattle were too expensive to be comin' up short in a count. And Pete needed more good help. He offered me the job of foreman – said it was Jane suggested it. It was mighty temptin' to stay on at the Circle R, no question about that. But I'd already made up my mind.

"Maybe sometime, Pete," I said, "It'd be great to be workin' here, all right. But I'm goin' to get at farmin' for myself. I've got my mind set on that. But before I settle down to that, I've got to find someone I'm lookin' for.

"Ferret Watson?"

"Well," I explained, "He's one of the people. But he's not the main one. I've got to locate a girl named Marguerita Hernandez." I told him as best I could about her.

"After that," I went on, "I'm goin' to settle into some nice mountain valley that's got enough water to raise crops, maybe stuff I could supply to minin' towns, or maybe if I find a place with a good road into Denver, I'll ship food there. I've heard about the valley north of here, Poncha Pass and up beyond there."

Pete, he agreed that might be country to look over, but I could see he wanted to come back to talkin' about Marguerita. "The girl you're lookin' for, Krieger. We'll go over to the bunkhouse, talk to Slim Carruthers – he's the older cowboy picked you up when you rode in. Slim's spent most the past five years out on the trail, movin' cattle – he was with the Circle R long before I came. He knows the inside of every bar two hundred miles in every direction. Slim's a born talker, and he drinks too much sometimes, but he learns a lot about everyone. What he says you can depend on."

After supper we went over there, and Pete was right. We sat on the corral fence and Slim pulled out cigarette papers and rolled one while he thought over the story I'd told him about Marguerita. He was quiet 'til he took a long drag, and he was thinkin' it over, I could see that.

"I heard that story afore," he began. "Never knew it was true, though. All us heard it kinda like a tale from a book. These two fellas had a woman with them, she couldn't talk, and she was a sort of witch, or so they said, could cast spells and the like. They kept her prisoner sort of, never brought her to town, made her keep camp for them. And they...they shared her. You know..." He paused, embarrassed, but we knew all right.

"These fellows supposed to've claimed she was an Indian they found east of the mountains, by herself, and they just took her along with them. They were drifters, gamblin' mostly, I guess. I heard once the girl'd been put up as the stake in a poker game. Somethin' like that.

"But Krieger, I tell ya, until tonight I thought those stories was just barroom jabber. Ya know how cowboys git when they've had a few drinks – they make up stuff to tell about, and ya can't tell whether it's real, like now, sometimes it's goddawful. A woman bein' treated most like an animal. It ain't right."

Slim stopped a minute here, and I was hangin' on what he still had to say. He knocked the ash off his stumpy cigarette, then went on.

"Krieger, I heard tell you shot Tinker Barclay last fall. That true?" Slim'd give me his piece of information, now it was my turn, I figured. I understood how Slim found out things.

"You heard right, Slim. He held me up while I had a summer's worth of gold in my pack, and I shot him. But his partner, Ferret Watson, he shot me and took the gold. Some day I'll catch up with him.

"That's the story I heard, all right. That Ferret Watson, he's a slippery one." Slim paused a second and looked across the fence at me, then he went on. "If you was to look for him, I'd bet you might do good to look up to Trevorton, the other side of Cochetopa Pass. The way I heard it, he's got a cabin up there now – most likely bought it with your money. Don't guess I'd expect to find any of that money left, though. Ferret, he likes liquor, gamblin', and women, not necessary in any particular order.

"'Bout the girl. I'll keep my ears open. There's way to find out more. From what you said 'bout when she was took, I figure they most likely hightailed it back into the San Juans. If they come out, they coulda come back over Wolf Creek, or they coulda come up into the Gunnison country – there's plenty of work and lotsa gamblin' up in there. I find anything about the girl, how kin I locate you? You go from here to Trevorton after Ferret Watson, you'll most likely be stayin' at the Bonanza. I find somethin', suppose I get word to you there."

Well, it wasn't all that much, but it was a start, and I was mighty obliged to Slim Carruthers. Just as Pete and I were about to go back to the house, Slim come up with a final word.

"Don't know how true this is, Krieger, but in the stories I've heard about the girl, when she gets kidnapped, Trigger Watson's usually one of the men took her. Sounds like him, but I can't say that it's true. Pete's likely told you we figure it's him takin' our cattle, but we've got no proof o' that neither. He's a lousy gunfighter, and a first rate bum, but he's pretty slick when he's sober.   You ever tangle with him, don't trust him no more'n you'd trust his no good brother...I find out anymore I'll let ya know up to Trevorton."

When we talked there on the corral fence, I had no idea, nor did Slim either, that Ferret Watson had the key to the whole thing.   But if it wasn't for Slim Carruthers I'd likely just have killed Ferret Watson when I found him and never learned the rest of what he knew.

CHAPTER 5

It wasn't' much to count on, but it was more than I'd had before, and I was sure Slim Carruthers had been talkin' straight. So the next mornin' I saddled Tempter, and with Polly lolly gaggin' behind, I took off west across the dry valley floor. I sweated ridin' across that trail to Saguache, but once I made my way up into the mountains beyond Saguache, followin' the trail that goes up along the stream bed toward Cochetopa, it was cooler and easier on the horses.

Along the way, I took time out to look for gold. I went up Jack's Creek, and some of the other canyons. There was color here and there, but I never found nothin' worth concentratin' on. And finally, maybe I'd been out from the Circle R ten days or so, I realized my mind was just on other things, so I rode down off the west side of Cochetopa Pass and into the valley east of Gunnison, and found Trevorton was a minin' town that had yet to have a real mine, but seemed to makin' it all right anyhow.

When it settled down, Trevorton was gonna be top ranch country from what I'd heard. But everyone said the winters up here were too long for the valley ever to be much for farmin' crops, and that's what interested me.

When I rode into town it was late in the afternoon. I took the horses to the stable and went across to the Bonanza. If Watson was here, I still had to find him, and I wasn't for him seein' me first. I got me a room in the front, overlookin' the main street and went upstairs to think it over. I'd been sittin' in a chair, my boots up on the window sill, for maybe half an hour, wonderin' how I'd go about locatin' Watson, when there were footsteps down the hallway, and there coma knock on my door.

I didn't figure Watson could possibly have known I was in town. Still, I walked across the room quiet, and I had my Colt in my hand.

"Yes?" I asked.

The voice on the other side was kinda breathless, and he spoke quiet, so the rest of the hotel couldn't hear.

"Mr. Krieger, I'm Waco Martin. I come from Slim Carruthers." Openin' the door slowly, I looked out and there was a kid standin' there, could hardly be more'n seventeen. He was a skinny kid I remembered havin' seen in the bunkhouse at the Circle R. I wondered how he knew I'd checked into the hotel.

"Mr. Chalmers, he told me you'd be here sometime, and the message Slim give me was important, so Mr. Chalmers said I was to stay right here near town, check the hotel every day, and don't leave 'til I talked with you." I could see the kid felt that what he had to say would be pretty important to me, and as he started out, his eyes got wider.

"Slim, he said to tell you, Mr. Krieger, and to be careful to tell you right, that before you shoot Ferret Watson, you'd best ask him about the girl. Don't never kill him before he talks. Slim said Watson knows somethin'." The kid stopped and looked across at me.

"How the hell did Slim find that out?" I asked.

"I don't know, Mr. Krieger. Ole Slim, he finds out lots of things. He has friends all over, and well, he just finds ways of knowin'." He paused, then he looked at me, somewhat wide eyed. "Mr. Krieger, you sure enough goin' to shoot Ferret Watson?"

I told him I didn't know, not that there was any question about if he deserved it. But I figured now I'd just have to see how it worked out. Getting' information about the girl was a lot more important to me than killin' Ferret Watson. But I still thought I could likely do both.

The kid wanted to leave. "Well, sir," he said, "You sure don't need me. I'll get on back to my cattle. Me and Tex Truman has a bunch of heifers on west o' here, and they're getting' pretty anxious. But Mr. Chalmers, he said to wait 'til you got here, no matter what, and I'm sure glad to've found you before...well, I'm glad I found you."

His footsteps went back long the dark hallway, and I heard him goin' down the stairs to the outside. I went over and sat down on the chair near the window, put my feet back up on the window sill, and went back to thinkin' about how to find Watson. I wasn't even sure I'd know him when I saw him. Only time I'd seen him was in the bar in San Badillo, and it was dark there. But I could remember his eyes that kept movin', lookin' everywhere but at me. The other time we'd met, he was behind a log, and all I saw was the glint of his rifle barrel – and I didn't see that quick enough.

It's funny, though, sometimes you have problems, like findin' Ferret Watson, and they seem like they might be hard to get answers for. You chew on them, then they solve themselves without any help. That's what happened with me and Ferret Watson. After breakfast the next mornin' after Waco Martin told me what Slim Carruthers had said, Id' gone across to the stable to check on Tempter and Polly. I was about to walk back across the street when I saw the sorrel horse, tied to the hitchin' post in front of the Ten Gallon Bar.

The horse was carryin' a fancy saddle, almost new, somethin' that cost a lot of money. Behind the saddle were my saddlebags! There was my K reverse K brand on them. They were the ones had the gold when Watson stole it. Why he ever kept them, I never figured out, but seein' 'em saved me a lot o' trouble.

The liveryman was oilin' some tack back inside. "That sorrel horse out there," I asked him. "That's a good lookin' animal. Know who owns him?"

"Sure," he said, "I sold the man the horse a few months back, when he came to town. He had a lot of money then. I doubt he'd sell him, though, if that's what you're after. Besides, mister, that sorrel's no match for your gelding – but I guess you know that."

"You said he had a lot of money when he came to town? He doesn't now?"

"Well, the man's a gambler, so his luck's sometimes good, sometimes bad. Mostly his seems to be bad. He came to town, bought that horse, bought a cabin out west of here – nice place fixed up pretty fancy."

"What's his name?"

"I suppose you can choose one, likely, and it'll fit. Men like him don't put much store in names from one place to another. But around here he's called Ferret Watson."

The liveryman looked across at me. "Say, you want to talk to him, he's probably over in the bar, and'll likely stay there all morning. He usually goes back home afternoons, then comes back to gamble at night. If you're thinkin' of gambling with him, though, I'd advise against it."

The liveryman just didn't have much trust in Ferret Watson, but then he wasn't alone in that. I asked him how to get out to Watson's cabin.

"He bought the place ole Cal Harmon built, but guess you don't know where that'd be. It's two miles outta town on the south side of the road, alongside Chieftain Creek, with a nice grove of cottonwoods. Watson don't seem to do much work on the place. Guess he's too busy losin' money at the Ten Gallon."

He was right. The cabin was a pretty enough place. I looked it over, then continued maybe a hundred feet beyond, 'til the cottonwoods were tight enough to hide me from a view of the house. I moved into the woods and tied Tempter to a tree, then walked back to the cabin.

There were no horses in the corral or the stable, but there obviously had been, and no one had dunged it out for the past month or so. I took a look up the road to see no one was comin', then walked across to the cabin door, kicked it open, and moved inside. The whole place was a mess, hadn't been cleaned for a long time, just like the stable.

Lookin' around, there wasn't much to interest me. Watson certainly wasn't a homebody. I sat down to wait. The sun was past overhead when I heard hoof beats comin' into the yard. I kept back in the shadows but watched out the window.

It was Watson, all right, and his sorrel was still carryin' my saddlebags. Watson was by himself. He unsaddled the horse, slapped her across the rump so she'd go on into the corral. Then he closed the corral gate, shouldered the saddlebags, and came back toward the cabin door.

Takin' a quick look up the road, I saw no dust from anyone else. When he came in, I was standin' across the room from the door, and my Colt was already in my hand. Watson shoved the door open, walked into the darkened room and dropped the saddlebags before he noticed me standin' there. I talked quiet, but sure.

"Don't reach for that gun, Watson! Just sit down in that chair there. You and I need to palaver a little."

He froze, then he recovered some and slowly raised his hands away from his gun. I stepped over and took the six gun from his holster, spun it open and dropped the cartridges out, then tossed it onto the bed across the room. I pointed again to the chair drawn up to the table.

"There!" I said. "Now!" Watson was scared all right, and he sat down. His eyes had gotten used to the dimness of the room and he looked across at me. It was the first he knew me.

"Krieger!" His voice was kinda shaky.

"Right, Watson, it's me. You left me for dead at San Badillo, along with your partner, Tinker Barclay, who really was dead. And you ended up with all this, with my gold." Tell you the truth, I was kind of enjoyin' it now, and I needed to get at him gently somehow about the girl.

"Tell me how you've spent my money, Watson." I sat down across from him at the table, but I turned the wooden chair around so the back was close to the table, and I holstered my gun. Sittin' backward like that on the chair, if I had to reach for the Colt, he could see it'd be a quick draw.

"Krieger, I..." Watson was in the chair, maybe five feet across from me, and he was leanin' forward, his hands on the table. "I...well, I spent most of it. It's about all gone."

He said it as if he was apologizin', as if maybe I'd expected to get it back.

"Tell me some of the things you've done," I asked him. "You must at least have had some fun with it..."

If we talked, I figured Marguerita's name would come up natural like and I'd maybe find out what I needed to know about where she was. If it didn't work out like that, well, there were other ways. Watson began slow, and as he talked he was kinda hesitant, like he was tryin' to guess why I hadn't just shot him. But as he remembered some of the good times, he warmed up to his storytellin'.

He'd not been talkin' more'n half a minute before I knew he was hidin' a Derringer in his belt. It wasn't like Ferret Watson to take no chances, I shoulda known that. I figured he'd keep talkin' while he worked on some way to get at that Derringer.

"I spent the winter in the valley, Krieger. I kinda moved along from one town to another. I lived pretty good, and I bought me the best horse I'd ever had – though the sorrel out there in the corral, he's a better horse even than the first one. You know, Krieger, I never amounted to much..." His voice was kind of whinin' now, and I hated his guts even more.

"Your money made me important. I drank, I treated at bars, I had a woman now and again. Mostly I stayed away from gamblin'." He went on, dronin' about towns, the good times, and I wanted to beat his face to nothin', but I held back, waitin' to hear about Marguerita.

"By spring I knew I wanted to come up here, get a place and just sit back a while. I bought this cabin, and I began to gamble in town. Once I went down to Saguache, thought maybe I'd start up some sort of business. There was a bunch of my old buddies from the Circle R. I bought them a lot of drinks, and we talked over maybe rustlin' some cattle from the ranch –

least wise, I did.   They didn't seem interested.

"I rode back up here, and stopped to do a little gold huntin' along the way, but I ain't got your luck, Krieger..."   He was feelin' sorry for himself, and maybe that helped him feel he deserved havin' gotten my gold because his luck was so bad.   I didn't buy that. He rambled on a while and I just sat listenin'.

"Krieger," he said finally, "Why the hell you want to know all this for?"

While he'd been tellin' those stories, I'd had my eye on him good. He'd edged his chair back, away from the table a few inches. He still had a piece to go, though, before he could reach the Derringer and swing it up in one movement. I was tired of the game now, so I came out with it.

"The girl you had, Watson..."

He laughed, nervous like.   "Which one, Krieger?   I had lots in the last year. With your money."

It was hard to hold onto myself here. He was getting' me all fired up angry, and I knew that's what he had in mind, that maybe he'd have a chance to draw if I got mad enough. I wasn't happy it was me had to bring up the question of the girl. I wished he'd done it, but it was too late for that now.

"The Mexican girl, Marguerita."

"Mexican? I ain't never had a Mexican woman, Krieger. Not up here nor in the valley either one. What're you getting' at?"

I realized then that maybe he'd never even known her name. She couldn't tell him.

"The girl who couldn't talk, Watson. You had her – I know that." It was getting pretty thin here, 'cause Slim Carruthers hadn't told me all that much. But I'd had to take a chance.

"I know you got her, Watson, and I want to know what became of her."

He had that Derringer in mind, no doubt of it. But I was hopin' he wouldn't reach, not until I'd learned about Marguerita. But I didn't much like the way he slid back from the table a bit more, still keepin' his hands right on the table, though. Then he settled down and began to talk, and I felt some easier.

"Oh, her, she was an Indian, not a Mexican. Least wise, that's what the fellas sold her to me told me."

"SOLD her to you?" I pounded my hand on the table, and my stomach was tightenin' into knots, but I knew I had to hold on here. I was learnin' now. He went on.

"Yeah, I bought her from my brother and a friend of his. They came up from Durango, they needed money and we worked out a deal."

I still didn't know what I had to, but when I understood what he was sayin', I almost shot him right there. That sonuvabitch had bought Marguerita, and he'd done it with *my* money.

"Trigger and the other fella, Todd Hunter, I think his name was, they said they found the girl east of the mountains, and they just brought her along. They bought a horse for her, they claimed. She limped some when she lived with me. Tell you the truth, Krieger, I think Todd shot her in the leg once when she tried to get away from them. She wasn't hurt much, though.

"I never did know whether she could talk, least wise she never talked when she lived with me. She could hear, though, and understand me when I told her things to do. Hunter and Trigger, they wanted to get over the mountains, down to the San Luis Valley, but they'd been down on their luck – they didn't even have money for food, and one of their horses was in a bad way. We got to drinkin' and they told me their story and, well, I just bought her from them"

I was havin' a hard time, tryin' to keep my anger from showin'. "Where's the girl, Watson?" I asked him.

"Krieger, what do you care about some Indian whore you likely never even seen?" He was probin' now, probably tryin' to get me even madder, thinkin' of that Derringer, and I knew it.

I just said "Talk, Watson!" He was back now with the chair to where when he wanted to grab the gun, he could. But I'd no thoughts that if it came to that, I couldn't outdraw him.

"I lost her in a poker game at the Ten Gallon Bar in town."

Well, I was shoutin' at him now. "Watson, dammit, you're talkin' about a human being. How can you gamble away a person?"

"I just did, that's all, just like I bought her." Guess he figured if you had money, you could just buy a woman, and if you'd bought her, no reason you couldn't sell her. Just like a horse or a cow.

"These two fellas, I don't even know their names, they'd stopped by here once to ask about an extra horse I had. I'd seen them in town, and they were gamblers. It was out here they saw the girl. A week or so later, after they were here, I got into a game with them. I don't know if it was rigged, or if I just had a run of bad luck, but I ran shy on money.

"The one said he'd settle the bets for the girl and the horse. I was kinda tired of her by then anyhow. There's just so much you can do with a woman can't talk. She's only company in bed, and it ain't hard to get plenty women of that kind. So I said she was theirs. Next mornin' they come by and she went off with them. They had to tie her into the saddle, but she rode off and I ain't seen her since. Krieger, that's the truth."

I could see he was tensin' up, but I had to know more. "Where'd they go from here, Watson?"

"I ain't sure, Krieger. They talked of Sunshine Pass and down to Alta Vista. There's lots goin' on there, and that was back in May and the Pass was just openin' up."

That's all I learned. Watson, he stood up suddenly, kicked his chair over backwards, reached into the belt for his Derringer and started to swing his gun hand toward me. But I'd been watchin' and waitin' for him, and he hardly had the Derringer loose from his shirt when my Colt caught him full on. It made a hell of a roar inside that room, and it shook dust off the ceilin'.

Watson got shoved backward by the bullet, and he shouted, "Krieger!" Guess it was part terror, and maybe some pleadin'. But it was too late then to do any pleadin'. He died without another sound.

I was so mad I never even gave a thought to havin' just shot a man. Lookin' down at him lyin' on the floor, I put my gun back into the holster and walked out into the afternoon sunshine. I slammed the door behind me, went down the road to the cottonwoods, still so mad I scarce knew what I was doin'.

Untyin' Tempter, I swung aboard. When we came back toward town, I stopped at the cabin again, dismounted and dropped the reins on the ground. Walkin' into the house, I looked over once toward Watson, lyin' there dead, picked up my saddlebags and walked out and threw them onto Tempter. I headed into town to pick up my gear and load Polly for the trip over Sunshine Pass.

Later, when I calmed down some, I knew I had to find some way to thank Slim Carruthers. Without him and Pete Chalmers, I woulda just shot Ferret Watson and never asked any questions. What there would be over Sunshine Pass, I didn't know, but from what Ferret Watson'd said before I killed him, I was at least headin' in the right direction.

CHAPTER 6

When I topped out on the pass, I stopped a minute and looked out to the west. There were mountains about as far as I could see. When I realized there must have been dozens of mountains out there that no one except maybe an Indian now and again had ever set foot on, I felt some idea of what a giant country we were livin' in, and how much we still had yet to find out about it.

But it was too cold to stay up there long, even if it was summertime. There were snow banks along there still, and I could see that little pond below the summit still had a skim of ice on it from last night, and it'd be thicker come mornin'. While I was enjoyin' that view, to the west I could see out there was a stack of clouds buildin' up, and I figured I'd best get on down the east side before dark.

We worked our way down across what passed for a trail. It didn't amount to much, and it took us most of an hour to ride down across that scree without gettin' ourselves killed by loose rocks. I was happier when we reached timber, and the horses was, too.

Soon's we got into the lodgepole pine, I started lookin' for a spot off the trail where we might camp. I heard a creek splashin' off to the south, and there was a grove of spruce alongside it. That would give us a lot more protection if it came to that, than the skinny lodgepoles we were ridin' through.

It was already pretty dark when we rode into the spruce, and I never noticed the tiny fire, nor the man sittin' beside it. When he spoke, my hand went for the Colt, but I never needed to draw the gun, for his voice was soft, and there somethin' about it that settled me.

"Join me, friend," he said. "It's a good place to bed down."

I looked carefully then, and I made him out. His dark clothes just kind of blended into the tree trunks. Inside a ring of stones, the fire was mostly hot coals, and a coffee pot sat above it, held up off the fire by some stones. He never stood up, but when I got off Tempter and walked over to him and he looked up at me, I saw his face was wrinkled and burned dark by years o' livin' up in this high altitude. I liked him right away.

When I travel I usually like to make camp by myself, but once I saw this old man, I felt no threat from him. I figured, too, he might know about people in these mountains, maybe about Marguerita. If she had been brought over Sunshine Pass, then her and the men who had her must have come down that same trail I'd ridden along, right past where I was campin'.

There was no way of my knowin' then that my meetin' up with this old man as it was comin' on dark would change the whole rest o' my life. I thought he was just another prospector hooked on gold, and we'd go our ways next mornin' after sharin' the campfire and maybe coffee. It wasn't like that, though.

Puttin' the horses over in the meadow beyond the spruces, I checked them to see whether the steepness and the roughness of the trail over the pass might have rubbed either one sore, but they seemed to have managed all right. A mule, hobbled, was grazin' a few feet from where I left the horses, and he eyed Tempter and

Polly like he didn't think much of them. A roan horse was back in the shadows, grain'n on the skinny grass grows up there.

Walkin' back over to the fire, I began to unroll my soogans and to start work on my supper.

"My name's Christian Pollock," the old man volunteered. "Most folks just call me Chris. I prospect up through here, and have a cabin down below, near Alta Vista where I hide out in winter. But summers I mostly wander around in these mountains. I just came back up the trail today with new supplies. Better have some of my coffee, it's just fresh."

He spoke well, like he was used to bein' with others. Some of the old timers I knew who lived in the mountains alone and never saw anyone else, they got pretty queer. But Pollock never seemed like that.

"I'm called Krieger," I said. As so often happened on account of the stories about me and gold, I thought I saw the old man's eyes raise toward me, as if he wanted to say he knew who Krieger was. But he kept silent, smokin' at his pipe.

We'd only been sittin' there maybe five minutes before he said, "Those clouds that've been buildin' toward the pass, they're movin' on in here, and it's goin' to come down hard pretty quick. I'm goin' to move me to a place I won't get stormed on. Whyn't you hike your things up with me and have your supper up there. We'll stay dry as tinder."

Looked to me he'd known from the first he was goin' to move out o' the rain, but he wanted to check me out to see whether he should invite me along. I must have passed muster all right.

"There's a cave not more'n a hundred feet up the canyon there, just the other side o' the stream, and about twenty feet up the side of the cliff. I've stayed there many a night before, and there's a good trail I built up to it. Come along."

He'd already begun to gather his duffel. I had half a notion to stay put, but I didn't like the looks o' that storm any more 'n he did. So I covered my saddle and as much gear as possible with my slicker and a tarp I carried, then I rolled up my soogans, gathered my food, and moved off into the darkness followin' along behind the old man.

When we got there the rain was just startin' up. Chris lit a match, and found some bark shreds at one side of the cave and got them burnin'.

"Last time I was here," he said, "I remember stackin' some wood in the back here somewhere." He found a few pieces and tossed them onto the fire. He'd known exactly where to build the fire, 'cause it was out of the rain but the smoke curled up the outside edge of the roof and went on up the cliff. The floor sloped some down so the rainwater that spattered on the outer edge ran off. It was pourin' down outside and I don't know when I'd been better protected.

"Off to the south there," Pollock said after we settled in a little. "That's the slope of Apache Mountain, and I'll tell you, in a storm like this with lots o' lightnin', it's no place to be. I was almost on top two years back, right after I first came here, when a big storm come up durin' the daytime. If I'd have had any sense, I'd a hightailed it outta there, but I kept diggin', and of a sudden my hair stood on end with lightnin', and a big round orange ball come up where a bolt hit. It rolled down the slope right past me. Smelled like hell must smell. My mule got knocked down, and when he got up, he was already runnin' down off the mountain. Took me the rest of the day to find him. I know there's mineral up there, but I just avoid bein' there again."

While I was cookin' up some bacon and some potatoes, Pollock got the coffee pot back on the fire. I saw he was eyin' me curious, and finally he said, "Lookin' at your pack when you come in, I see you've been a miner. You said you were named Krieger. You the fellow I heard about they say finds gold easy?"

I laughed. "Well, I found some, I have to admit to that. But easy or hard, I don't know. Stories you hear aren't always true. I've no great urge to find the stuff, like some people have, but on the other hand I've never complained about having money."

"You countin' on prospectin' up here?" he asked me.

I told him I might sometime, but first I wanted to look at Alta Vista. "I've been travelin' since I was fourteen," I said, "and it's time I took roots. I heard Alta Vista might be a good place for that. I lived on a farm in Pennsylvania, and I think right fondly of farmin'. If I got a chance, and if the ground was right, I'd think of tryin' it here. It's not the same as Pennsylvania, I know that. But I've got some itch in me that says to grow things. First, though, I've got some other things I need to get done." I was aimin' to get the conversation away from me, so I could head it toward Marguerita.

"Looks as if this country up here would have a chance of developin' into big, year 'round hard rock minin'," I suggested.

"Not for me, it won't," he said. "This here eastern slope gets too many avalanches. I come up here once two years back, mostly I just wanted to see what it was like winters. But I'll never come back in wintertime. I couldn't even see this cave, it was so full o' snow. The whole mountainside behind here just let go, and settled into the gulch. I don't scare easy – that time in the 'lectric storm over on Apache, and then up here in the winter. I was scared then, all right. I just tiptoed back outta here on my snowshoes and went back to town and enjoyed the rest of the nice winter we had.

"Might be gold's got its hold on me in the summertime, but winters it would take somethin' more'n gold to get me up here. I found my share over the years, and I could sit down in my cabin in Alta Vista 'n never come into these mountains again and I wouldn't starve. I've got maybe the best piece of land in the valley, a section with plenty of water, and grass up to your shoulders, and I don't do nothin' with it 'cause I'm up here durin' the summer, huntin' the yaller stuff. Maybe it's I like the outdoors.

"Maybe, too, it's I got no one else cares if I'm alive or dead, so I bring my loneliness up here to share it with the wild. I was married once, back in Illinois, and we come across in a wagon, like everyone else. She didn't wanta come, she loved that black soil in southern Illinois. She had a baby in the middle of a Sioux raid. Both her and the baby died. Then I lived with a Cheyenne woman a long time, out east o' where Denver is, but she's dead now. Like you, I figured to settle into Alta Vista, and in a way I have, but somethin' keeps urgin' me into these mountains."

He broke off the conversation by walkin' to the front of the cave and lookin' out. "Clearin' off, I guess," he said, "like it always does. Big storm sweeps through, then it clears off sweeter'n anything you've ever seen." He stirred up the fire a little and added a couple of logs from the pile inside the cave. Pollock looked like a man I could trust, and I needed to keep the conversation movin' so's we could get to Marguerita.

"You up here off'n on all summer, then?" I asked.

"Yep. I've got a claim right down below here. The claim includes the cave – you'll see the stakes out there in the mornin'. I do enough work to keep the claim alive. Back in the end o' the cave I've got a kind o' rocker stored. I can carry it down to the streambed by myself, and it's better'n pannin', specially at my age. The placer's good, but I'd put it for sure that some real minin', up the canyon walls, would tap into a vein of hardrock. But I guess I'm too old to be shinnyin' up walls, blastin' rock, and diggin' tunnels. What I find up here now's as much as I need, maybe more, and I guess I'll just continue to enjoy summers up here 'til my legs or my lungs won't get me this high any more. Then I'll sit in front of the cabin down in Vista and soak up some of that clear mountain sunshine. I ain't lookin' forward to it, but I suppose there must be worse things."

Sittin' there in the flickerin' light, I looked across at him and wondered whether I maybe might end up wanderin' the mountains, still workin' a little placer here and there. At twenty four, I knew it was hard to think of bein' maybe seventy, but I had a goal now, and I saw myself as a successful farmer, part of a town somewhere, and with a wife to love. I reckoned I could manage all that.

Looked like maybe I could bring up Marguerita now. "Pollock," I began, "you've been around here some time, and you're up in these mountains all summer. I need to know about someone you might have heard of. I'm lookin' for someone."

"What's his name?" he asked.

"It's a girl. Her name's Marguerita." I wished it was lighter so I could see his face better.

"Never knew anyone that name, sounds Mexican."

"Well, she was stolen away from a Mexican family that saved my life once, but she wasn't really their child. They found her after an Indian battle down this side of Taos. She was the only thing left alive in the camp. They took her home and raised her as their own 'til she disappeared more 'n three years back.

I saw I had him interested. He leaned forward. "Who would have stolen a girl?"

"Two saddle bums came across her when she was herdin' sheep. Trigger Watson and Todd Hunter were their names."

"I heard of Watson," he said. "Claims to be a gunfighter. What makes you come this direction lookin' for the girl?"

I explained how she'd been sold to Ferret Watson.

"Sold her?" he said. "To his own brother? You can't sell a girl, even an Indian. Krieger, we just fought a hell of a war mostly about that."

I agreed, but then I went on. "Ferret Watson kept her prisoner and used her bad, and finally he claimed he sold her to two other men early this summer, and they were maybe headed over Sunshine Pass."

"Where's he at, Ferret Watson?"

"He's dead," I explained. "About a week ago I killed him."

Pollock never said a thing. He got up and walked to the edge of the cave again, looked into the darkness, came back and sat down and sucked on his pipe a little.

"Krieger, this girl would be maybe sixteen, seventeen, now? She's been through a lot of hell."

I agreed with him, and added, "I don't know what she might be goin' through right now, with those two bastards who bought her. I don't know where to look, except the vague notion she was brought over the pass."

The old man leaned toward me, his eyes lookin' hard at me in the half light from the fire.

"Krieger, this Marguerita, you called her. She couldn't talk, could she?"

I'd been leanin' back but I jumped up and grabbed the old man by the front of his coat and pulled him closer to my face.

"My god," I said, "you know about her. Tell me, dammit!"

"I think I know her," he said. "She must be the same one. But first, leggo me. I can't breathe when you're holdin' me like that. What's this girl look like?"

He had me there. I'd never seen her, and Juan and Maria's description was three, almost four, years old. Who knows what might have happened to her durin' that time? I couldn't tell him much.

"She Indian, though? Thin, kinda willowy like? She's tall for a woman, most 'specially for an Indian?" They were really all questions he put to me.

"Pollock, I just don't know. Her father said she could ride a horse as if she and the animal was the same, could shoot a gun better'n most men, and was born understandin' more about animals 'n anyone he'd ever seen. But I can't tell you what she looks like."

I'd lost patience with the old man, and I told him so. "Pollock, tell me what you want to tell me about her – get on with it. And if somethin' happened to her…" I let it trail out, for I didn't know what I would do if somethin' had happened to Marguerita, just as I was findin' out about her.

Pollock, he was really interested in the girl, all right, that was clear enough. But he was interested in his chance at story tellin', and I'd not time to sit through it all, not without findin' first whether she was alive.

"For God's sake, Pollock, just tell me first. Is she alive?"

"She's alive, Krieger, she's in good hands – maybe better than you could ever imagine. She's not with those two men you talked about, not any more. Now let me git on here."

Well, I'd learned my lesson, and I'd found out the most important part, so I sat back and he went on at his own speed.

"Sometime," he said, "after all but the last of the snow was off the trail this spring, two men come over from the west. I never seen them, but there's always a good bit o' travel soon's the trail opens up across the top.

"Joe Danforth, he's a mule skinner in Vista, and he figured to be the first over the pass, even if it took a lot o' work. He loaded up with food and supplies they might be short of in Trevorton, and had two of his mules heavy with whiskey kegs. He'd broke his way over the pass, shovelin' part way so the mules could get a foothold. He'd got into Trevorton, unloaded and sold his stuff. He turned right around and come back up the pass. He no more'n topped out and started down this side, he come across these fellows and the girl.

"They more or less tried to hide her, least wise they tried to hide how she was tied to her saddle. But he seen it. Joe didn't really pay much attention – not 'til later when he thought back on it after..." Pollock left the words hang, but I kept my mouth shut. I knew the story would only take longer if I asked questions.

"Joe recalled they never come through town that he saw. But he figured they'd maybe gone to prospectin'. None of us even knew that part about Joe seein' them 'til afterward. A week, maybe ten days, later, Mike O'Malley and his wife, she's Erla, they was comin' up the trail to the pass, plannin' a little early fishin' in some of the high lakes that'd just thawed out. They were only a couple miles this side o' town when they saw her.

"She was on a scrawny pony, a little mustang, hell bent down the trail, ridin' bareback, though she did have a rope on the critter. When she saw them, she rode right up to them, motioned to them with her hand to follow her. They asked her questions, but she never said nothin', just kept motionin'. Finally, they was still standin' there on the trail, and accordin' to Mike, she reached over and grabbed the bridle on Mike's horse and started back up the trail, draggin' his horse along with her.

"There's not much Mike's scared of, you'll see that. He was carryin' a rifle along, too. So they followed her. She turned up a draw to the north, back into where there was a grove of aspen along a stream. A camp was all set up there, with a tent, and a fire goin', with pots and things. And there was the two fellows, dead as could be, both shot through the head.

"Best I can find out, don't seem clear exactly what happened. Doc Train, he rode back up there with Mike afterward, and they decided the men shot each other. The sheriff, he never even took the trouble to look the place over, he agreed with Doc Train. But 'course it's possible the girl mighta shot them both – I'd never a blamed her, for she musta been pretty bad treated.

Anyhow, Doc felt he'd better say the men shot each other, and the sheriff didn't much care.

"They was known in Alta Vista, they'd been around last summer – some more of those bums we have wanderin' through that work at odd jobs if they have to, drink the rest of the time, and aren't worth a hoot."

He'd had his story, and I'd have to hand it to him. He told it good. But I was impatient to know the rest.

"What's become of the girl, Pollock?"

"She's been kind of adopted by the O'Malleys. They never had any kids of their own, so when the Indian girl came on them, and they went through this whole thing with her, they took to her. So she's livin' with them, and they call her their daughter. They named her Colleen, never knew if she had another name 'til they discovered she could read 'n write. Then, after they found she was named Marguerita, they still thought Colleen was prettier.

"She got scrubbed up, Krieger, and Erla made her new clothes and Mike bought her some fancy Indian duds in

Denver.   Mike bought her the most beautiful pinto pony he could find, to replace that bony critter she was ridin' when she found them. You know, in just those two months she's been with the O'Malleys, she's got to be about the most beautiful creature I've ever seen. Krieger, can you imagine an Indian named Colleen O'Malley?"

It was clear the complications were pilin' up for me. I somehow hadn't thought of it happenin' like this. I figured I'd find the men who stole her, maybe have to shoot them, and I'd return the little girl to Maria and Juan. Of course I should have known she would have grown into a woman now. And it just never came to my mind she'd be adopted or taken by someone who would love her, like the O'Malleys seemed to. This would take some thinkin' on my part.

Pollock wasn't finished yet. "There's some wonderment in Alta Vista about the girl, as if she had some kinda special powers or somethin'. Showin' up in the mountains with those two dead men, and there's still some feelin' that maybe she shot them. Not that it matters to me, they deserved it all right. But her bein' Indian, that don't sit well with some people down there. There's lots o' folks hate Indians, no matter what. Way I look at it, they killed my wife, and that weren't right. But we was killin' them and takin' their land. We did more'n our share to get rid o' them.

"The O'Malleys, they intend to treat her like their own. Anyone in town don't like that can deal with Mike, and that'll take some doin'. If you've a mind to take her back to the people she lived with before, you'd best go in to Mike O'Malley with guns ready."

"I'm not about to do that, Pollock. On the other hand, I don't know what's right. I'll have to think on it some. The most important thing, though is that we know she's alive and in good hands."

Pollock settled back into the darkness, and I could see only the glow from his pipe as he drew on it. I was tired of talk and ready for sleep when Pollock spoke up again.

"Krieger, if you've a mind to get in minin' again when you settle into Alta Vista, it might be a good thing to think about comin' in with me. This valley'll give us our share of gold, I'm pretty sure of that. But it'll take more muscle and more brains than I have. If you've a mind to, we can talk it over sometime after you've looked over the town and settled that about the girl and the O'Malleys."

What he said was mighty surprisin', and I'd have to admit I was pleased the old man had accepted me so quick.

"Pollock," I said, "I sure thank you for your offer. I maybe might take you up on it, but I gotta get the other things straightened out first."

I heard him knock the ashes out o' his pipe, and he said, "Think on it, Krieger. No hurry."

The embers were burnin' down, and I could see the stars just above the top of the ridge across the valley. There was a lot to think on, all right.

CHAPTER 7

By the time I got Tempter saddled up and loaded Polly, daylight was beginnin' to show down into the canyon. I thanked Pollock and rode on back to the trail. As I went down toward town I was studyin' the land pretty careful 'cause it looked as if I might settle down in these parts. The trail went along Topaz Creek, and I could see that even now, most the end of summer, the creek was still runnin' nice. The snow hadn't yet melted clear off the north side of the mountains.

One place along the trail, still pretty high up, I could ride out on an edge of rock. Lookin' down I could see the valley below me was full of beaver ponds. That late snow cover and those beaver ponds would even out the stream flow where it came through town. The slopes off on my left faced the sun and were all seared brown, and most of the trees where runty pinons. Off to the right, where the snow piled in there was some big old ponderosas, and every little canyon on that side had a trail of aspen comin' down toward Topaz Creek.

The sun was close to straight overhead when I got down to the chalk cliffs. They went clear out to the entrance to the canyon. I'd heard about these in travellin' around, and it was excitin' to see them. The rock on these cliffs wasn't hard, and it had been washin' away. Some parts must have been tougher than others, 'cause there were pinnacles stickin' up, and some had their sides eaten away here and there, so there were caves.

Someone who'd been here once told me the early Spaniards were supposed to've come up through the San Luis Valley and explored this northern valley, and found the mountain I was in now was full of gold. They were supposed to have hidden the gold in caves in the chalk cliffs because it was too heavy to take clear back down to Mexico with them.

From what I'd heard, though, no one ever found any of this gold. It didn't look to me like the Spaniards would have been stupid enough to hide their gold in those caves up there, 'cause they looked as if the next storm might wash them away or block them up. If I'd been goin' to hide gold I'd a put it into some of the hard rock caves, like the one Pollock and I had spent the night in.

Below the chalk cliffs I stopped and looked out across the town to the east. The canyon opened out into a broad, flat plain that slipped off smooth toward the east. I knew from a map I'd seen at the Circle R that a lot of streams flowed out onto this plain. But Topaz Creek, which I'd been ridin' down along this mornin', was the biggest.

From the map, I remembered seein' that on the east side of the plain where I could make out a low ridge of rough mountains, the Arkansas River had cut itself a channel. I knew the Arkansas from two, maybe three, hundred miles farther east. It dropped down from here and went through a big sharp canyon for almost a hundred miles.

From a book I'd read once when I was with the wagon train, I remembered readin' how Captain Zebulon Pike come up that canyon way back in 1806, lookin' for a way west. But when he got to the mountain range I was comin' off now, it was winter, almost Christmas. He and his men thought better of it, went back down the Arkansas and found them a way south. He ended up clear down in Santa Fe. These mountains were just too much for them in winter, and from what Chris Pollock'd said last night, I could understand.

There was a road went straight across the plain, and I figured this must be the stage road to Denver. It was more'n a hundred miles across there to the city. North, maybe fifty miles, there was a boomtown they had started to call Leadville, where there was a strike goin' on.

Lookin' down on Alta Vista, to me it looked like most other towns. It had maybe a prettier location than most, 'cause Topaz Creek ran along the south side, and I could see the town would catch the winter sun, but because it had the chalk cliffs behind it, it'd ought to get some protection from the winds. The trail slanted down off the ridge I stood on, straightened out and was the main street through town.

There wasn't room for Alta Vista ever to be a great big city, and that suited me right. If it grew too big it would have to grow out onto the plain below. Pollock's cabin, from what he'd told me, was down there on the little road that cut from Alta Vista north and met up with the road into Leadville that come up along the Arkansas. North of his place, he'd said, was the Hoover Ranch, a big spread of grazin' and hay land.

Swingin' Tempter and Polly back to the trail, I come back down to the west edge of town. From above I'd noticed the O'Malley livery stable was on the south side, maybe half way into town. I already knew from Pollock that O'Malley was in Denver and would be there the next three or four days.

But the hostler who was runnin' the place while Mike was away gave me a stall for Polly and Tempter and I unloaded Polly. I left Tempter saddled while I went over to the hotel, the Senate, and got myself a room. It was a nice enough hotel, with a café and bar alongside, called the Mother Lode. Like most of the towns in the Rockies, the buildings were bein' added to, includin' the hotel. Pollock'd said there were no real big strikes yet, but lots of interest, and towns often live more on interest than on ore.

I came back and untied Tempter and we rode out east. I was anxious to look at the plain, for I figured that's where there might be farmin' ground. When I found the trail north, I swung up in that direction. It was better'n a trail, less than a road. There was plenty of sign it was used for cattle, and wagons could manage, at least the part I rode on. It wasn't exactly the Santa Fe Trail though, not yet anyway.

Pollock's cabin was west of the road on a little plateau maybe six feet higher'n the creek that came down past it. Where the ford was, I stopped for Tempter to drink, then we rode up the trail to the cabin. The old man had chosen well, no doubt o' that. From up there I could look clear across to the ridges off in the east. West, the slope was gradual up through a ponderosa stand. A band of aspen clung to the creek bed down a tiny canyon right back of the place.

On the mountains up high I could see a series of openings like fingers, came down through the trees. Avalanche paths. But they were way up high, no problem to Pollock's place.

I wished was me had got there first, for this was the place I'd been dreamin' of. When I looked out across the plain I could imagine irrigation ditches, and I could figure what crops I might try raisin'.

But I had to learn more about the valley. Startin' down the trail from Pollock's cabin, I noticed a dust cloud maybe a quarter mile south. Looked to me like someone was movin' cattle through, so I waited among the cottonwoods 'til they passed – I didn't want to spook the cattle none. There were maybe fifty head of yearlin' heifers, and a few old cows. A tired old cowboy was ridin' point, holdin' them down to a walk. He never even noticed me.

Those cattle were top grade. They had that same look about them Circle R stock had, white faces with a little range blood worked into them, just a little stringier, a little tougher lookin' than the Herefords they'd started bringin' straight from England. The cowboy ridin' draw seemed in no hurry. He stopped to water his pony in the stream, movin' a few feet up beyond where the cattle had crossed, and rolled a cigarette while his horse drank.

I rode out of the cottonwoods. "Nice lookin' cattle," I said. "You from the ranch up north of here?"

The cowboy looked me over pretty careful. "That's right, the Double Circle Double H, the Hoover place." He stopped, took a drag on his cigarette. I don't think he was sure whether he ought to go on, but he must've decided maybe he could get more information than he could give, and word about strangers would always come in handy.

"You just goin' through?" he asked me.

"Don't' know," I said. "might stay a while in Alta Vista. Rode out here to take a look at Pollock's cabin. Came across him in the mountains a while back. Sure has a nice location."

"Don't do much with it, though. He's gonna sell out pretty quick now, I expect."

Sell out? I wondered. Pollock'd not said anything about sellin'. He'd been talkin' about sittin' down here on the front step when he got too old to climb the mountain any more. From what I'd seen of the place, if he was interested in sellin' out, I'd be talkin' with him.

"Surprisin' he'd sell," I said. "I thought he intended just to retire down here sometime when minin' gets too much for him."

"He's got more water'n he knows what to do with here. My boss needs it. He's goin' to buy the place." The tone of the cowboy wasn't much to my likin'.

"He talk to Pollock about buyin' him out?"

"When the time comes, Pollock'll sell, all right. What Mr. Hoover wants, he gets. He's a powerful man, Hoover is." I couldn't explain rightly, but that cowboy's talk set my teeth. What he was doin', it seemed to me, was threatenin' old Chris Pollock, and I didn't take much to threatinin' anyone, specially an old man like Pollock.

The cowboy jerked the reins, lifted his horse's head, and spurred the animal into a trot as he went up the trail, catchin' up with the heifers that'd moved on up ahead. He said simply "See ya!" and he was gone.

Makin' my way back to the crossroads I turned east across the plain, puzzlin' over what the cowboy'd said. The country was as beautiful as any I'd ever seen. I watched a band of antelope who were wary of the sounds of Tempter and me. They edged off to the south. Above the road off to the east, a bald eagle wheeled around in the sky.

I was moseyin' along, enjoyin' the flat open country, when I heard behind me the sound o' horses runnin', and voices. I turned around and watched the dust cloud grow closer, and the sounds increase. Funny, I thought for a minute of Indians, and reached down to check my Colt. Ute hunters had been up in this valley for hundreds of years. I knew that. But I also knew the white man had forced them out some years back.

When the riders got closer I could see half a dozen children ridin' scroungy lookin' ponies at full gallop. They were havin' a great time, shouting to each other, and I drew Tempter off the road, out of their way. They waved as they passed me. I thought back on my own growin' up, and I was pretty envious of these kids. After the dust settled, I got back on the road and followed the kids on east.

It was late summer, but the Arkansas was still carryin' a load of water. I figured if it was high now, then durin' spring runoff the ford must be impassable for days at a time, at least to wagons or the stage. Even now, the water reached up on Tempter maybe a couple feet, and he stepped careful account of the current. By the time I'd started back from the hill country to the east of the ford, the afternoon shadows were stretchin' out pretty good.

I'd come only a few minutes west beyond the river when a girl on a piebald pony raced in from the south across the flat toward me. I remembered seein' the horse with the band of youngsters that galloped past me on the road. I checked Tempter and waited for her.

She was still some distance away, pushin' her pony hard, when she shouted at me.

"Mister! Mister! We need help. We were fishin' and foolin' around down the river. My little brother, Otto, he fell in and got washed downstream. Can't none of us swim, and he's holdin' on a rock or somethin'. He lets go, there's a big whirlpool down below and he's a goner. You help?"

I spurred Tempter, and the girl and I raced back through the rabbit brush toward the river.

"I hope we're gonna make it," she shouted. "Otto's just a little kid, and that water's 'bout cold as ice."

As we got closer to the river I could hear the rush of the current. The other kids were standin' along the bank, shoutin' at the boy. The river had narrowed there, a lot narrower than up at the ford. I looked out, and the kid wasn't more than twenty feet from the bank. But I had no rope, and obviously none of the kids had either. He seemed to be holdin' to a ledge of rock, or maybe it was a tree trunk – I couldn't see anything under the water. He wasn't very sure of what he was holdin', and his legs were stretched out from the rock, pulled downstream by the current. It was pretty wild water on both sides of him.

While I was sizin' it up, I got off Tempter and unbuckled my gun belt. The stream was really roarin' through that narrow area there, but down below where the kid was hangin' on I could see it got even narrower and there was a drop off. The waterfall was maybe three or four feet high, and there was a kind of bowl below it. That was trouble, that bowl. The water'd be swirlin' and twistin' through there.

But on the far side of where Otto was, it looked to me like there might be some backwater, and if we could get in there we'd make it all right. I dropped the gun belt, ran maybe forty feet upstream to where I figured the current would let me swim out to the boy. I shucked my boots as I went, and I dove in.

The girl was right, that water was icy cold, and it hit me like a board in the face. My whole body drew up complainin', but I kept swimmin', fightin' to get my breath. I wondered how that damned kid had held on all this time. He must have been froze. It looked like I judged pretty good, and I was comin' down on Otto from upstream. I figured the current was goin' to swing me right to him.

If I could get hold of whatever it was he was holdin', I'd get a breather, get him to grab onto me, and we'd have a chance to get set to fight our way into the backwater on the other side before we'd be swept down into the waterfall. It all went good enough at first, but just as I moved up to the youngster, he got panicky and reached out for me.

He lost his hold and the current shoved him downstream away from me. It took all I could do, but I reached out for him and got a piece of his shirt and held on. Trouble was, by the time I got him, it was too late to kick into the backwater. We were in the main rush, and bein' swept down over the drop.

The current rolled me over, and I grabbed the kid to me, held him in a bear hug, protection' his head with my arm, and I doubled myself up best I could. Our only chance now was in goin' clear through the whirlpool and driftin' into the quiet beyond it. For the moment there was no point in fightin' the current. It was a damned sight stronger'n me.

We spun over the drop, went through the bubbles on top, and got shoved right to the bottom of the river. I felt a rock tear through my shirt and into my shoulder. We were rolled over again, and the back of my hand, holdin' the kid's head, scraped over a sharp rock on the bottom. But there was a second when there wasn't too much current, and I pulled my legs up under me and felt my feet on the bottom. Still holdin' Otto, I sprang upward 'cause my lungs were hurtin' bad. That maybe saved our lives, for I got a fresh breath before the current sucked us back down. I couldn't tell about Otto, he was just hangin' on.

We got spun around to the bottom. Again down there the current let up for a couple of seconds and I kicked us toward the surface. We were already through the worst, and I felt our way to the rocks at the edge of the stream, where the water was some shallower.

When Otto and I got ashore the other youngsters had got down there and were waitin'. I looked down at him. His lips were mighty blue, and his whole body was shakin', but he smiled up at me, and I knew he'd make it.

While we were still in the water I shouted to the kids to build a fire, quick. And when I got up the bank, I told the two nearest ones to grab Otto and hug him tight. I knew that would warm him up faster'n anything else. I looked over at the kid, still bein' grabbed by his brother and sister. His color was some better, but he was still shakin' so bad all three of them was vibratin' up and down. He moved over to the fire, and so did I.

"I sssssure ddddoo tttthank you, mister," he said through his chattering teeth.

"What's your name, son, other than Otto?" I asked him.

The girl who'd galloped up to me on the piebald, and who had the matches to build the fire, said simply, "We're Muellers!"

She never said "We're the Muellers" or "We're the Mueller Family." I didn't know for a minute what they had to do with mules, but then it came to me that was their name...Mueller. Back in the German part of Pennsylvania I'd lived in, that was a name there was a lot of.

I guess they figured anyone around Alta Vista ought to know Muellers. I let it go at that, but I didn't know then that their daddy would sometime be a pretty important man in my life.

It was comin' on to sundown before Otto was warm enough that they all mounted up and galloped back toward home. They thanked me again, nice enough. I let them run on ahead, holdin' back Tempter. The air finished dryin' my clothes and I walked Tempter back up to the Denver road.

Fifty miles away, off to the south, the Magic Mountains were still hangin' in that kind of twilight there is out here, and I watched as the long round wind clouds turned the color of a peach, and then, very quick, the light went off them. Pushin' Tempter into a trot, we rode on back toward town. The ridge of mountains at the west side of the valley had the sharpest peaks in them I'd ever seen, except maybe the Tetons. There was just a glimmer of light left in the sky above the peaks, and a star, bigger'n any star I'd ever seen, hung there right above the highest mountain.

Somehow or other this was goin' to be the place I was goin' to live.

CHAPTER 8

After I'd had breakfast at the Mother Lode, I'd decided I'd walk around town a bit. I hadn't got very far before a short, fat man walked up to me.

"Excuse me," he said, and when I heard his accent I remembered back to Pennsylvania. I'd forgotten most the German I grew up on, but he reminded me in just a couple of words of that whole world I'd run away from.

"Excuse me," he said, "but are you the man who saved my Otto's life yesterday?" By now he was shakin' my hand, and I admitted as how I was the man.

"When the children came home from their ride last night, they told Momma and me how Otto would have drowned if Katrina hadn't found you on the road. I want to thank you, Mr. Krieger, for me and for Momma – and for Otto. And I want to tell you we welcome you to Alta Vista. And the Muellers, we hope you stay here."

Well, it was sure a nice speech, and I got a kinda lump in my throat. I couldn't remember ever bein' thanked like that. Nor had anyone ever welcomed me to a town, or even asked me to stay on, either. I'd already decided I wanted to live in Alta Vista, and now thanks to this funny fat little man, I began to believe that maybe the town wanted me. It was a good feelin' all right.

The next couple of days I spent lookin' the town over and ridin' into the mountains and out east of town, mostly waitin' for Mike O'Malley to come back from Denver. Not that I knew what I was goin' to say to the O'Malleys, 'cause every time I thought it over I never came up with how to go about it.

Ridin' into the mountains, I found this was mineral country, no question about that. I panned a few of the creeks and found good color almost everywhere, but I had to admit my mind was more on the girl than on gold.

Comin' back to town from the Sunshine Pass trail, I rode Tempter up behind the stable and tied him to the rack to cool him off and brush him down. I walked inside to get a curry comb, and didn't see the hostler anywhere around.

But once I was inside, I heard what sounded like a fight goin' on in one of the empty stalls. At first I thought it was some kind of animals, then it all of a sudden turned out to be people, a man cursin', and what sounded like fists. I moved over to the stall. My eyes were getting' better in the low light. When I got to the front of the stall where the noise was, there was a gun belt lyin' there.

In the straw was where the fight was goin' on. I'd a figured it was just a couple o' kids, except for that gun belt. I didn't like it. Walkin' into the stall, I bent over and grabbed the man nearest me by the pants, lifted him up and shoved him to the back of the stable. The bottom figure rolled over and got part way up.

My God, it was a girl! I could see her face was scratched, the front of her buckskin shirt was ripped open, and the roundness of her breasts was clear. There was no question she'd been in a helluva fight, and I could hear her breath comin' hard. She slowly stood up, tryin' to fix her clothes. She looked at me like she thought maybe she was goin' to have to fight me, too. She was an Indian girl, and I just knew she had to be Colleen O'Malley.

The man at the back got to his feet and never said anything. He just come at me. He was movin' pretty fast and he knocked me clean into the aisle as he rushed past the girl. I could see her move toward the open door at the back of the stable, out of our way.

He was maybe my height, but I had fifteen pounds on him. As we fought I could see he was a youngster, probably about eighteen, and he wasn't yet filled out across the shoulders or in his chest. Still, he was a handful. I wasn't sure how serious all this was, not until he gave me a shove and reached down for the gun belt lyin' on the floor. Then I knew it was no foolin', and I set off to finish it.

Soon's I saw what he was after, I outguessed him. He took the pressure off me for a second to go for the gun, and I pushed forward. As his hand reached toward the gun I stomped it, hard. He caught his breath as the pain rocked him, and gave up the gun at least for a minute. He stormed into me but I had him now, and once he'd tried for that gun, I knew I had to finish him off. I drove him back into the stall, poundin' his face, and he buckled slowly against the posts, then collapsed onto the floor. I could see his nose was smashed and runnin' blood pretty bad.

He wasn't goin' anywhere for now, so I backed out to the openin' to the stall, reached down and grabbed the gun from its holster, spun it open and dumped the bullets out. What was left of a coal fire was still burnin' in the forge where the hostler must have been workin' on horseshoes a few minutes back. I dropped the gun in, pumped the bellows a time or two 'til the hot coals sparked, then I walked out the door to the girl.

She'd been bruised up pretty bad, but I doubted she'd been hurt serious. Lookin' at her clothes, I figured she'd not been raped. No question, though, it was a matter of minutes before she would have been. She was shaken up all right, but lookin' at the fire and anger I saw in her eyes, I wasn't sure whether the kid I'd left in the stable would ever have been able to get done what he started to do.

Lookin' at the girl, I was astonished, for she had none of the heaviness of the

Utes I'd seen down south of San Badillo. She was tight muscled, thin, and she eyed me like she was a princess.

We stood there lookin' at each other for a few seconds because I didn't know what to say, or even whether I should say anything. Finally, I loosed my neckerchief, dropped it in a water bucket standin' outside, and handed it to her. She took it from me, kinda bowed slightly, and then smiled at me, shy like. I knew she was sayin' thanks, though there were no words.

When I heard the man in the stall startin' to move, I left Colleen and walked back toward him. He was getting' to his feet, pretty wobbly, and when he saw me he started to rush me. I grabbed him and shoved him.

"Not so fast!" I said, "or I'll knock you down again."

His head seemed to be clearin' pretty quick now, and he put his hands up onto his bloody face. He favored his right hand, the one I'd stomped on.

"Damn you!" he shouted at me. "Who the hell are you anyway?"

"I'm named Krieger, sonny!" I couldn't resist that last word, for I remembered myself at his age, and there'd be no greater insult than my callin' him "Sonny", me bein's just a little older than him. There was maybe only six or seven years' difference in our ages. He glared at me and stood straighter.

"The next time," he said, "I'll kill you!"

"The next time you try anything with that girl, I'll not let you off," I answered. "Instead of just a mashed face, you'll have a bullet through you. There are laws. You can't treat other human bein's that way."

"Aw, she's only an Indian whore."

After what that girl had been through, and none of it her fault, I was in no mood to listen to this kid. I grabbed him by the shirt and was ready to pound him again, but I let go, disgusted, and I shoved him away from me.

"What the hell's your name, kid?"

"None of your..." But before he could get more out, my anger got the better of me, and I moved in and backhanded him hard across the face. It must have hurt like hell, what with his nose already bein' smashed.

"Tell me your name!" I shouted at him.

"I'm Tim Hoover," he said quietly. "My old man's Brady Hoover, and he'll kill you for this!"

"He always fight your battles for you?"

Still holding his face, but ignorin' me, the boy walked past me to where the gun belt was. He picked it up with his good hand, and discovered his six gun was missin'.

"Where's it at?" he asked.

"I don't figure it's safe to give it back to you," I said, "but if you really want it, hold on..." I took a poker, fished the gun from the forge, and dropped it on the floor in front of him. It was red hot, and the heat had twisted it some. The butt was clean burned off.

"You sonuvabitch!" he said. He left the gun there, turned and walked out the front door, yankin' it open so hard its hinges squeaked. I watched him go, then walked to the back of the stable. But Colleen had disappeared. I'd never seen anyone like her, and just lookin' at her, I knew my search had been worth every bit of it. I went to brushin' Tempter, for I had a lot to think about now.

CHAPTER 9

That night I was havin' supper in the Mother Lode when two cowboys came in. They took a good look around the room, and when they saw me they gave me a pretty good goin' over, then turned and went into the bar and ordered whiskey. That older one, I recognized him as the cowboy was ridin' point on the cattle were bein' moved up past Chris Pollock's place. They were Hoover men, and I figured they had their eye on me, all right.

There was only one other man in the dinin' room. He was off to one side, a little behind me. I couldn't tell whether he'd paid any mind to the cowboys. I ordered a drink and my dinner, and was sittin' there workin' on a piece of steak when the outside door came open and a lone man walked in.

He was tall, thin, his hair was goin' gray, and he had a narrow, grizzled kind of mustache. I figured him to be in his forties, too light to be much account in a fight. His face was flushed from too much liquor over the years. His clothes, well, I never wore clothes expensive as those. He looked like maybe a rancher, but a little too flashy. He could have been a gambler, I suppose. Least wise if he was a rancher he had enough hands workin' for him, he didn't dirty himself with the chores.

He went on into the bar and I saw him talk with the two cowboys had eyed me. Then he came back out, walked toward me. I kept my hands above the table – can't say I much like his looks.

"Krieger," he said. "I'm Hoover. You thrashed my son this afternoon and I intend to kill you."

Well, I had to give it to him. He talked tough, and I had the feelin' he might try carryin' out his threat.

"Hoover," I said, "if your son had been a man, I would have shot him. I don't believe in women bein' raped, and that's what he was at. And before you say it, I don't believe in white women or Indian women bein' raped. It's against the law, and you can tell him if I ever see him at it again, I won't be so easy on him."

Hoover, he just stood there lookin' at me, and I went on. I was beginnin' to get pretty riled up with him. "As for shootin' me, maybe we'll have a go at it, but only if those two monkeys over there put their guns up on the bar. Fair's fair. I got nothin' against facin' your gun, but I'm not countin' on workin' on a whole army."

"Hank, Spike!" Hoover motioned to the two men at the bar who'd been watchin' us. "Come over here!" They walked toward us, their guns still holstered.

"Krieger here is gonna draw on me,' he said. "You see it's all fair." That was a joke, and all four of us knew it. If there was gonna be shootin', I'd never have a chance his way.

But then the man at the rear table spoke up. He must have been watchin' us quietly. He had a voice with plenty of authority, and I turned my head around when I heard him.

"Hoover! Krieger's got more sense'n to draw with the three of you standin' there. Now, get out of here or I'll kill the lot of you. From what I heard of this afternoon, if it had been me discovered Tim, I'd have shot him cold. Krieger just taught him a lesson. I hope the kid'll remember it. I patched up his face as best I could, but it will take a while to heal. And his gun hand is going to be out of the game for a long time. Maybe that will save his life sometime."

The man had never moved from the table where he was sittin'. He just sat there, the Derringer in his hand, his hand restin' on the table. None of us had even noticed when he drew. I figured that at that distance Hoover had no options. For him or either of his two men to draw would be askin' to die. One might make it, and kill me, but two would most likely die. And none of the three of them knew which two would end up dead. Hoover's hands were half raised now, far from his gun.

"Doc," he said. "I won't forget this!" He jerked his head toward his henchmen, turned and strode out the door.

When they'd gone, the stranger behind me tucked his gun back into his belt and walked over to my table.

"I'm Doc Train," he said. "I think you'd better buy me a drink."

"Seems the least I can do," I answered, "seein' you maybe saved my life, Doc. They were kinda stackin' the cards against me. Sit down here." I shook hands mighty warmly, and Doc pulled out the chair opposite me.

"I don't really think Hoover would have killed you," he said. "But with three guns as possibilities, I thought the odds were a bit high. I hope you didn't mind my interfering."

"Hardly, Doc, but I didn't think the whole town would be in on the little fracas this afternoon."

"Don't guess they are, yet. But they will be before long. Doctors are something different, though. Erla O'Malley came running down to my office, yelled for me to come look at the girl. It was pretty obvious what had happened to her, or had been about to happen. Nothing really did except she got beaten up some. I was just walking back to the office when Tim Hoover ran up, his face bloodied up. You hit hard, Krieger..." He looked over toward me and laughed, then continued.

"I patched him up, and I put two and two together, but got only about three and a half until this evening. Then it all made sense."

I liked the Doc straight off. Maybe it's not hard to like someone who's just put himself on the line for you, but Doc had a way about him seemed right to me. In spite of the trouble we'd just been through, he was a mighty relaxed fellow. I couldn't imagine he'd ever tackle anyone in a fist fight – he was skinny, only medium tall, and his voice never sounded tough, just sure. But where there were guns, I figured he'd count. But like tonight, he thought mighty quick, and that's the best way to stop a gunfight – before it gets started.

"Krieger," he said, "I doubt that Hoover or his gunmen will tackle you again, at least not right soon. But you can bet that Hoover will never forget you, and neither will his son. If you're planning to stay around Vista, I guess it will be at your own risk."

"Well," I said, "I've been around other places on the same basis, Doc. It might not seem it, but I'm really a peaceable man. I just don't like seein' people wronged. I'm not one to hunt trouble, but I don't much run from it most times when it shows up. Fightin' isn't always what's needed, but mostly it seems to work out that way for me. Hoover and I, we'll manage."

"You're thinking of staying in Alta Vista then?" He was curious about me, and had no reason not to show it. On the frontier your curiosity about people pretty often has to be a bit limited. But Doc musta thought, and he was right, that if he'd helped me stay alive, and if I'd called him a friend, then he had certain rights. I begrudged him nothin' – fact is, I wanted to talk some about my plans.

"Doc, I've been movin' since I was a fourteen year old, when I ran away from what was supposed to be my home. I've been to hell and gone most places in the west. But if you want to know the truth, I've decided I want to be a farmer. A just plain dirt farmer. I'll run a few cattle maybe, but that's ranchin'. What I want to do is raise crops, maybe some chickens and hogs.

"'Course, I know it'd be a sight easier back in Illinois or even Pennsylvania, where I came from. But I've kinda taken to the frontier, and I figure as people move in here, there's goin' to be a need for food."

That seemed to make sense to Doc, 'cause he agreed with me. But then he wanted to know what had brought me to Alta Vista. I thought that one out a while before I answered. Sometime, I had to talk with Mike O'Malley, but it would be easier to have someone arrange all that. I didn't know whether Train would be the right person, but I felt right off he could be trusted, and he had already shown he was friends of the O'Malleys and knew Colleen. I made up my mind.

"Doc," I began, "I've a story to tell you about what brought me here. But it has to do with a lot of people, some of them you know, and I think before I get wound up, we'd best be in more private surroundin's." I looked over toward the bar, which had picked up some customers by now. Doc was lookin' across the table at me, and it was pretty clear I'd got his curiosity up.

"Fair enough," he said. "Let's walk over to my place up the street. Who knows, I might even have a patient waiting. Besides, my coffee's better than Sing Lee's – I think he makes it with rattlesnake bones."

Doc was right about the patient. Outside the office there was a woman holdin' a bundled up baby. She was sittin' on a bench up against the wall of the house.

"I told you, Krieger," he said, and he turned to the woman. "Hello, Samantha, come on in." He walked into a hallway in the middle of the building, opened a door on the right, struck a match and turned up a lamp. It was his office.

"Be right back, Samantha, soon's I get Krieger here settled." He motioned me to follow and walked on down the hall into what turned out to be the livin' room. When he turned up the lamp, I could see a kitchen in the back, another room off to the side, probably Doc's bedroom, I figured.

"Make yourself at home," he said. "I can provide a little Taos Lightnin', but I'll get the coffee I promised after I tend to my patient." He turned and went back up the hall.

Pourin' myself a shot o' whiskey, I looked around the room and discovered the wall behind me was lined with books practically to the ceilin'. I'd been in a real library once or twice. In St. Louis I looked up some things about geology. But I'd never seen books like this just in someone's house. Back in Pennsylvania the only book

I could remember we had was the Bible, written in German.

On the table was a stack of books, and one of them was open. I took a quick look at it, but it wasn't even written in American. After I tried to reason out the words, I decided it had to be Spanish. I'd never seen a Spanish book before. I was still studyin' it, tryin' to puzzle it out, when Doc Train returned.

"Kid has a fever," he explained. "Not much I can do for him except maybe make his mother think someone cares. He'll likely recover no thanks to me, but her husband's up traipsing around in the mountains, looking for gold or silver or some magical way to make a living without working for it."

He noticed I'd been into his Spanish book. "My harmless hobby, reading. It keeps me out of bars, away from being shot by jealous husbands, makes me think I'm more aware of the world – though maybe that's not such a good idea at that…"

We settled down with coffee he'd been warmin' on the back of the stove. "You were going to explain to me," he said, "why you had come to Vista." He sat down on the couch, which was covered with a buffalo robe. I was already sittin' in a wooden chair that was across from him.

Well, I was still a little hesitatin', but I'd made up my mind I'd try my story on Doc Train, and we'd see where it all went from there.

"Doc," I begin, "I came here to find a girl, a girl named Marguerita Hernandez."

He stopped me. "Krieger, I know about every person's been here any amount of time the last three years. That's not a name I know. Tell me about her, though. I didn't know I'd be getting a love story!"

I got right to the point. "You know her as Colleen O'Malley, Doc." Well, that startled him all right.

"Colleen? You know her from somewhere else? Were you trying to find her?"

Doc listened while I told the whole story as quick and straight as I could, endin' up with how I found where she was, and killin' Ferret Watson. I told him, too, about runnin' into Christian Pollock in the mountains, and how it was Pollock recognized that Colleen was Marguerita

Hernandez. Doc never asked me was I sure the two were the same. By then he knew my story held water.

But all the time I was talkin', I knew Doc was thinkin' about the O'Malleys, and how important that girl had become to them. And like Pollock, he wasn't about to get involved in their givin' her up.

"You expect to take her back to the Hernandez family, Krieger?" he asked me finally. I figured I'd best put all the cards out, and I told him I didn't really know what to expect now.

"What I'd really thought, Doc, would be that after huntin' her, I'd find the bastards who stole her, would probably have to kill them, and then would simply take her back home. I guess I'd figured to be a kind of hero, and would have paid my debt to the Hernandez family for carin' for me.

"But, Doc, it's gotten a sight more complicated than that." I was hopin' I'd get him involved in all this – I needed help, that was certain. "I expect, Doc, that you and I are goin' to need a lot of bein' smart to know what's right to do."

There was another thing'd been botherin' me since I saw Colleen this afternoon. "Somethin' else, Doc. All these months I've been carryin' a little Mexican doll with me. It's somethin' she had at home in San Badillo. All this time I've been thinkin' of her as a little girl that played with dolls. But when I saw her this afternoon I had to shift all my thinkin'. Far from bein' a little girl, she's maybe the most beautiful woman I've ever seen. When she stood up, Doc, after I pulled Hoover off her, I saw there was no child left in her. I shoulda figured that, but I didn't, not 'til this afternoon."

Doc got up and poured some coffee, and then we talked some more. "Sometime," I went on, "I've got to tell the O'Malleys, but I guess I'd best be sure before I talk, what I want to say, particularly about the girl goin' back to San Badillo."

After he thought it over for a while, Doc suggested, "Look, Mike O'Malley ought to be up from Denver sometime tonight with the new stock. Why don't we discuss it tomorrow night at their house? I'll invite you there for dinner. Erla O'Malley cooks the best venison you'll ever taste. As a bachelor I never pass up a chance to sit at her table. And I know them well enough I can just invite you. It might be smart to get Alice Trimble – she's a teacher's been working with Colleen – to take the girl to her house for the evening so we can talk."

I appreciated Doc's bein' willing to get into this, and I could see no reason to put off talkin' with the O'Malleys, so we agreed on meetin' the next night unless there some hold up from the O'Malleys. I'd leave that to Doc.

It was late when he let me out the front door. The town was most all in bed, I figured. There was single lamp in the hotel down the street. But when Doc closed the door to his place behind me, it was dark on the street. I'd walked halfway across to the hotel when I heard the horses. They weren't far along up the street, and I knew they were racin' toward me. But from the sounds, they were separated, on opposite sides of the street. I was in the middle. Well, first I figured every town has its drunks, and I just kept on walkin'.

Then suddenly I could hear the rope singin', and it was singin' "Danger!" And it was danger for me. I dove for the ground, had my Colt out before I rolled onto my shoulder. The rope the two horsemen stretched between them whizzed over me, and the riders raced on down the street, their hoof beats getting' quieter off in the distance. My gun was no good, for I never even saw them.

Doc Train must've heard those horsemen, 'cause he came out the door and runnin' toward me. "Krieger!" he shouted, and I don't guess he could even see me. "Where the hell are you? You all right?"

"Well," I said as I picked myself off the street, "I'm a mite dusty, Doc, but at least I didn't get a broken neck. It's an old trick, but not one I've ever had played on me before. You know, Doc, I remember at supper you're tellin' me that Hoover wouldn't likely be botherin' me again tonight. But if I had to guess the corral those two horses are headed into right now, I'd put my money on the Hoover place."

"No bets," said Doc.

CHAPTER 10

Mike O'Malley was a giant. When he opened the door for Doc Train and me, it seemed he filled the whole doorway. He was tendin' toward too much weight, and after I'd sampled Erla O'Malley's cookin', I saw his problem. But when he moved across the room I saw he handled all that bulk well. He wasn't' exactly like an antelope, but then he wasn't a bowl of puddin', either. He was more like a grizzly, I figured. If it came to fist fightin', I knew it'd be handy to have Mike O'Malley takin' my part.

I wasn't sure how much Doc had told the O'Malleys, but he'd said to me they were expectin' to hear about where Colleen came from. That house had about the best cookin' smells I'd ever got, and Erla O'Malley came out of the kitchen to greet Doc and me. Alongside Mike, she looked pretty tiny, with chestnut colored hair and a nice rosy color to her cheeks.

"I wanted to thank you for yesterday," she began. "I didn't know what had happened to Colleen until Doc put me straight. That girl's had more than enough troubles, Mr. Krieger, without that, too."

"I'd o' been there," Mike O'Malley growled, "I'd o' killed young Hoover." He made it sound as if he'd have done it with his bare hands, and maybe he would have.

We'd sat down to the table and Erla O'Malley was passin' the food when Mike spoke up. "Doc tells us you know the story of Colleen, Krieger. We want to hear it all, even the parts that might hurt. But before you begin, have it clear she's ours. That wherever she came from, she's not goin' back."

His bushy eyebrows hid his eyes, but when I looked over at him, I knew he meant what he was sayin'. I didn't see much of a problem here, but decided I didn't want any, either, not with Mike O'Malley. His wife shook her head slowly in agreement with what he was sayin'.

Well, I went through the whole story once again, just like I told it to Doc Train the night before. All day I'd been thinkin' out what was right to do, and now, 'specially after I'd met the O'Malleys, I'd decided what I wanted to suggest.

"Looks like we don't have much of a problem," I said. "I'd agree that Colleen should stay here. But I think she ought to be told by you that you know where she came from and how she got here. I'll ride on down to San Badillo and tell her other family she's here, and that she's safe and happy. Sometime I think it would be good if Colleen could go back to see the Hernandez'. But it looks to me she needs more time to settle in here."

It all turned out easier than I'd figured. They agreed to what I suggested.

Havin' settled on this, we turned on to other things and like Doc, Mike O'Malley wanted to know what I planned to do. I'd been hopin' he'd bring it up, 'cause I wanted to talk about Christian Pollock, and find out what they had to say about him.

After I told how I was lookin' for some farmland near Alta Vista to settle onto, I said as how I needed time to do some minin' first, and that Chris seemed to have offered me a share in his claim. When I said this, O'Malley looked up at me surprised like.

"Chris Pollock?" he asked, then went right on, "Do it. He's a fine man, and he's about at the point he needs help. I don't know anything about the gold or silver might be up there, but Chris is honest and dependable. Those are two things you don't find in everyone hereabouts."

Doc, he nodded in agreement, then added, "Chris's in town, you know, came down this afternoon. If you want to talk with him, look him up in the morning, because he says he's going back to the claim as soon as he loads up that mule of his. Krieger, you'll never find a better partner..." He paused a minute so's I'd be sure to get what he was sayin', then he went on. "But look here, Krieger, don't be mucking around up in those mountains any longer than it takes to make a stake to buy land. There are lots of miners comin' in here, not enough farmers. The miners will get the headlines in the Denver papers, all right, then cause us a lot of trouble, take the money from their gold elsewhere, then move on. What we're lookin' for, Krieger, is people who will stay...people like you!"

Doc's voice made it pretty clear he was serious about that, and it gave me a good feelin'. When I looked over at the O'Malleys, they were both noddin' that they agreed. I remembered Hans Mueller the other day, and how he'd asked me to stay on in Vista.

"Exceptin' the Hoovers," I said, "this town's a mighty friendly place."

O'Malley shifted his bulk in the wooden chair, and leaned forward across the table. "Look here, Krieger, don't never underestimate the Hoovers. They're dishonest, sly, they believe in settlin' things with violence. You've not heard the last o' them. But if it comes to that, ye can count on us." Lookin' across the table at him I knew he was talkin' the truth.

Next mornin' I went to see Pollock. It was comin' on cool now in the early mornin' and I let Tempter have his head. I felt his enthusiasm as we galloped up the road. About half way up to Chris', I gentled Tempter down to a trot. There were three riders comin' toward me, and I could make out one was Brady Hoover.

Shiftin' in my saddle a little, I could feel the weight of the Colt in the holster. But I shifted my reins to my gun hand. I wasn't lookin' for any fight with Hoover this mornin'. I guess we felt the same way, at least for the moment, 'cause Hoover kept lookin' straight ahead, as if Tempter and me was never even there. I'd gone maybe thirty feet past when Hoover said, loud, "Krieger!"

That voice really riled me, like he was callin' his dog or somethin'. But I reined in Tempter gentle like and turned him sideways in the trails. He danced kind of impatient, 'cause he'd had his mind set on goin' ahead, and I guess I felt about the same way. Hoover had turned clean around and rode back to where I was. I'd o' been damned if I'd o' gone back to him.

"Krieger, you goin' to see Pollock? I noticed he's up there loadin' that mule o' his."

Never figured how he knew I was goin' to Pollock's. "I might be," I said.

"Well, you tell that old man I intend to buy his place, and I'll offer him a fair price for it. You tell him that, Krieger. My offer won't last forever. After that I'll get his land, and he might not like how I do it. You tell him that, Krieger, you hear?"

The hackles on my back were scratchin' me. He was talkin' to me like I was some cowhand of his, bein' ordered to get a pack o' chewin' tobacco. I leaned my legs against Tempter and moved him closer to Hoover, and I raised my reins in my gun hand so Hoover's boys wouldn't mistake that I was goin' to draw.

"Sure, Hoover, I hear you. And I'll give your message to Pollock. But I'd guess, if I was you, I wouldn't hold up here on the road waitin' for an answer. I doubt he wants to sell, sure not to you." And I swung Tempter back up toward the trail to Pollock's, leavin' Hoover standin' there.

When I came over the rise to the cabin, the old man was tightenin' the cinch on the packsaddle, pullin' the air out of that mule of his.

"Welcome, son," he said, lettin' up on the cinch for a minute. "All I hear about you around town is good things. Understand you fished young Otto Mueller outta the Arkansas, and saved our Irish Indian from pretty serious trouble. It's good to see you again, besides I'm wore out packin' this stupid mule. Let's sit down an' have a cup of coffee. Tie up that dun and we'll palaver a bit."

He brought out two mugs and a worn coffee pot from the house, and motioned me to sit on one of the giant ponderosa rounds was leaned up against the cabin. He sat on the other and poured the coffee.

"Doc tells me you made a mite bad enemy, too," he went on. "Them Hoovers, there's just somethin' about 'em I can't abide. Saw Brady goin' past a few minutes back. I'd o' spit on him, but at my age I can't spit that far no more."

"He stopped me," I said. "Gave me a message for you."

"I got the message a long time back, Krieger, and I've heard it lots since. He wants to buy my place. Why shouldn't he? I got the best land and most the water, water he can't do without. I wouldn't sell my place to him, even if he threatened to kill me."

"That's close to what he did, Chris. Said if you wouldn't sell out, he'd get your land anyhow, and you might not like the way he got it."

Pollock put down his coffee cup, and looked over toward me. "I'm an old man, Krieger, and my time might not be far away. His shortenin' it wouldn't make that much difference. But he better know I can still draw gun." He picked up his cup and took a long drink of coffee.

"Now," he went on, "I got somethin' more important to talk about, and it involves you. Word is you might be aimin' to do some prospectin', and I'm suggestin' like we talked the other night that if you're interested, you pitch in with me. I already got that claim up there, maybe there's somethin' worthwhile, maybe not. But the signs seem pretty fair, an' if after while you figure it won't 'mount to nothin', you can just walk off an' work somewhere else. But I'll make a legal arrangement with Lawyer Miller in town that we go 50 – 50 on my claim, and on any other we might find and work together.

"Look here, Krieger, I ain't no young chicken no more, and most the muscle work'll be your'n. We talked about it kinda, up in the cave. But now I'm offerin'. Doc Train says you'll do it. I found plenty color up there, but as yet I ain't located no hardrock to be worthwhile. Without that it's hard work and maybe not much real pay. I hear tell you almost smell gold, and if you're interested, let's get on with it."

The offer wasn't any surprise to me 'cause we had talked about it, and I'd thought on it a good bit since. Ridin' around when I was waitin' for Mike O'Malley to get back, I hadn't seen anythin' that just startin' out from scratch looked any more promisin' than that gulch up there by the cave. And in the meantime I'd found out Pollock was as good as his word, and I like that in a man.

"Chris, that sounds fine to me. You go ahead with the agreement, I'll stop by the lawyer's office and sign it. But one thing, you've got to know it'll be maybe ten days to two weeks before I can get up there with you. I've got to ride down to San Badillo and see the girl's folks – well, her other folks, anyhow. I promised the O'Malleys I was for their keepin' Colleen, but I at least owe it to the Hernandez family to tell them she's found and is in good hands. Eventually I'd like to see she gets back down there to visit, but she's got enough problems in her life right now."

"Sure, that'll be all right, Krieger. But we'll have to set to pretty hard, and I don't want to get us snowed in. One thing we'd oughta do, when you get up to the mountain, we'd oughta put a front on the cave, make it into a kind of cabin, so we could work up there later into the winter. My old bones keep arguin' for that, Krieger. On one o' my supply trips 'ta town I'll get us a little potbelly stove 'n pack it back up. That cabin'll have to be heavy enough and sloped so any avalanche comes down during the winter'll just slide off it. That'll take some buildin'."

Things got movin' pretty fast about here, but I felt Chris and I could hit it off right well, and I'd o' bet there would be enough ore up there for me, with my share, to find me a farm here in the valley by next year, maybe sooner. And when I was in San Badillo, I'd look into what was my share of the Ptarmigan Mine down there, too. I wanted that farm pretty bad, and already I was getting' an idea of who I wanted to live in it with me. I'd only seen Colleen O'Malley a handful o' times, but somehow now my thinkin' of the future always come back to her now. I'd have to see. That'd be a big step, and I had a lot of little steps to take before I faced up to that.

CHAPTER 11

Figurin' to be gone less than two weeks, I travelled light. With my soogan rolled with extra clothes and stashed behind me, and my slicker tied on top, I felt like a trail hand again, and both Tempter and me liked bein' out on the road again.

We found our way up across Poncha Pass, and we dropped down into the San Luis Valley on what had to be about the most beautiful trail I'd ever ridden. The Sangre de Cristos were off to the east, already snowcapped by an early storm, even earlier than the one caught me at the Ptarmigan Mine last fall. The trail was full of wildlife. On the pass there were deer almost everywhere, and I saw a handful of elk. One old bull elk was rubbin' his antlers against an aspen, shakin' those quakie leaves and bendin' and twistin' the trunk.

When I got down into the basin, herds of antelope were grazin' there, most like cattle. I put the spurs to Tempter once, and we chased a bunch of them just for the hell of it. But they wanted no part of us, and I brought Tempter back onto the trail. I thought of shuckin' the Winchester and takin' an antelope for supper. But I hate to waste meat, and antelope's no great favorite o' mine. Besides, they were so pretty out there, I'd been hard put to shoot one. Erla O'Malley'd packed me some strips o' venison, and when I made camp and warmed that a little, I figured there was nothin' better.

The second night out I was bedded down alongside a little pond just on the west edge of the valley. I watched two bald eagles soar in and land along the shore of a pond. One had a fish, and while I was watchin', the two eagles circled and danced around each other like a couple o' fighters. Somehow I found myself wishin' that Colleen O'Malley was along with me. I figured she'd enjoy watchin' those birds. But I guess there was more to it than that. Anyhow, I remember I went to sleep thinkin' about how she looked on that pinto of hers.

Tina and Antonio were in the front yard when I rode up, and when they saw me they let go with whoops. They recognized me right off. Antonio ran to the door of the kitchen shoutin', "Mama, Mama! Krieger's back!"

I got off Tempter and led him to the tie in front of the stable, and all the time the two kids were pesterin' me with questions. Maria came to the door, wipin' her hands on her apron, and she walked out the path toward me. She was shy, almost as if she was scared to talk with me.

She turned toward Antonio and said quietly, "Ride to town and get your father. Tell him Krieger has returned." The she turned back to me and said, "Welcome to our house."

Maria had about her a way of talkin' that made me feel it was somethin' special to be with her, and I reckoned that though Colleen wasn't even her real child, she had that same specialness. It gave them a kind of importance, somehow. Only in Colleen it wasn't anything she said, of course, it had nothin' to do with talkin'. It was just the way she looked, walked, and maybe 'specially the way she rode a horse. Of course, I'd not seen her more than a few times, but I knew about that all right.

As we walked in toward the house, Maria stopped, turned around and faced me. I knew now why there'd been that kind of hesitation when I first rode up. Almost in a whisper, she asked me, "Marguerita, you have learned anything of her?"

Knowin' how much she'd worried about the girl, I'd figured to tell her right off first thing.

"I've not only learned about her, Maria, I have found her!" I let that settle in for a minute, then went on. "She's fine, Maria. I couldn't bring her with me, but I will tell you all about her, and later on sometime she'll come down to visit with you. She had a hard time, I'll give you that. But you need have no more worries about her, Maria. When Juan comes, I will tell you all about it."

She was cryin' now. "Ah, Krieger," she said, "I knew you could be trusted to find her. You are a great man, and we will be forever in your debt."

Of course that made me feel right good, but it seemed funny to me too, I guess, 'cause it was her and Juan had saved my life.

"Come," she said, "You will stay with us. I cannot give you your old room, for we have a patient there. Seems almost as if we run a real hospital these days." She spoke proudly.

"Things go well with you, then, Maria?"

"Wonderfully, except until now I didn't know about Marguerita. To learn she is alive, there could be nothing better. I can only thank God – and you, Krieger."

We all had supper on the patio shaded from the evenin' sun by the row of cottonwoods west of the house. I'd been worried about how to explain Marguerita's adoption by the O'Malleys. But to Maria and Juan that seemed no problem, because they were so pleased I'd found the girl that nothin' else mattered.

Juan wanted to talk about the mine with me, and Maria was gone to look in on her patient, a youngster who'd been smashed up when he tried to cross a rock slide and brought an avalanche of rock down, with him in the middle of it all. "He'll get better," Maria had explained to me. "But he'll be badly crippled in the legs.

Maybe he will live here with us..." She went to look after her patient.

When we talked about the mine, Juan explained, "You know only one summer has passed. But my brother, Miguel, and his two sons have been living up there since you left. You were right, it is a big lode. By next summer we will have taken the money from this summer's work, and we will buy much equipment, and we will hire many people, and the mine will become important to the town San Badillo.

"You can take your money from the summer. We have kept it separate. Or if you want, we will put it back into buying the mining equipment. But by next summer at this time, you will be a rich man, Krieger. We will all be rich, and it is because you know where to find the gold, and because you were generous with your finding."

He wanted me to take a day and ride up to the mine, but there was somethin' pushin' me to get back to Alta Vista, and I told him I wanted to leave for the Circle R the next mornin', and maybe I could visit the mine some other time, because I was goin' to visit again.

Juan looked out into the hall to see that Maria was not yet comin' back, and I knew he had something else to talk over.

"While we are alone, I must talk seriously to you. Trigger Watson, the brother of the one you killed, he was here in town a little while ago. I have not seen him, but I'm told he knows you killed his brother. He says he intends to kill you when he finds you. I think he is not here right now, but Krieger, you must be careful."

"I have heard, Juan, that it was Trigger Watson who stole Marguerita from you. Him and a man named Todd Hunter."

Juan looked up at me sharply. "You're sure of this, Krieger?"

"About a man like Watson, it's hard to be sure, but it was his brother told me, just before I killed him. He had no cause to lie. But in any case, someday Watson's path and mine will cross and we will settle our scores. I felt it was right to kill Ferret Watson, and when I find his brother I will have no hesitation in killing him, too."

"Still, Krieger, you must be careful. He is not any ordinary gunfighter. He would maybe not hesitate to shoot you any way he could do it."

I left the next mornin'. I'd promised Chris Pollock I'd be back, at least that's what I told myself. But I knew it wasn't really Chris was botherin' me. I was thinkin' of Colleen O'Malley. So I headed north. I intended to get to the Circle R to stay overnight, then I was aimin' to ride straight on back home. Alta Vista, somehow, had already become home to me.

An evenin' with Jane and Pete Chalmers didn't even do much to stop my wantin' to get back to Vista. Pete was riled up about the troubles the Circle R was havin' with rustlers.

"We're losin' so many cattle it may ruin us," he explained. "The range country west and north of us is filled with our cattle, and even if we have cowboys and line riders, when we run a count we always come up short. At roundup this fall we'll know how many we've lost, but we already know it's bad.

"Worse, Krieger, the rustlers are getting bolder. Last month one of our cowboys out west was found shot. He must have discovered them at work, and they killed him. So far we haven't been able to prove who's doing it, but we will. I hope it's before we go broke."

We'd walked over to the bunkhouse to talk with Slim Carruthers. One thing, I wanted to thank him for getting' me the information about Ferret Watson. Carruthers sat on a bench out in front of the bunkhouse and rolled a cigarette as he talked.

"Best I can find out," he said, "our rustlin's likely bein' done by your old friend, Trigger Watson. He's been behind this all summer, ever since he came down from Trevorton. He seems to have plenty of money when he shows up in Saguache or someplace else, and no one knows where the money could come from, except from sellin' our cattle, and there's nothin' can be done 'til we catch up with him.

"And most important, we've got to find where he's takin' the cattle he steals. He's in cahoots with some big operator who most likely looks honest, probably has a ranch of his own, and can sell without raisin' any questions. We'll get to both him and to Watson, but looks to me it'll take a lucky break or two."

Pete nodded in agreement, and said gloomily, "In the meantime, it might be pretty tough around here. We may lose a lot more cattle, and worse, those rustlers may get more of our men."

When we walked back to the main house, Pete said, "Tomorrow, when you leave, I'll ride up with you and check the north camp. There're only two men there, and none of those late calves has been branded. We won't get an iron to them until we round up in the fall when we move the cows and calves to winter pasture. They're sittin' ducks for trouble up there."

It was right as we were fordin' Roundstone Creek, from what Pete had said maybe a mile south of the cow camp, when we heard the shots. There were three quick, distinct rounds, then there was a volley, all pretty much together, then there was silence.

Pete jerked up his stallion's head from where he was drinkin', started off up the trail at a gallop. I was right behind him on Tempter. That old horse could smell trouble, just as much as I could. And this was trouble, had to be.

"Let's get there, Krieger!" Pete shouted. We'd run maybe five minutes when Pete put his hand out to the side and slowed the stallion to a walk. I moved up alongside him.

"We're about there," he said. "The cabin's a hundred feet or so out into that clearing." I could look through the aspen and see the sunlight in the clearin'. There was a log corral just beyond the cabin, off to the left, with its back fence almost into the woods.

"Best we can do is ride up, keepin' to the woods, and be as quiet as possible until we see what's happening," Pete said, and he led off with the stallion at a walk. We worked our way up through the grove to where we could make out both the cabin and the corral clearer.

Only person we could see was a horseman, standin' in the corral gate, keepin' a small band of cows and calves inside the corral. Out beyond, on the ranch pasture, there was a lot of dust and after a second I could make out three, maybe four, riders movin' a bigger herd in toward the corral.

"Rustlers!" Pete said quietly. "They must have gunned down my men!"

I shucked my Winchester and began to lift it toward the cowboy at the gate. I wanted action quick. But Pete put up his hand and stopped me.

"Wait," he said. "The others will just scatter if you shoot now. They'll come in closer and we'll have some chance of getting the whole bunch. Let's ride on maybe another fifty feet or so. It'll be an easier target then." We rode on up, keeping inside the aspen grove.

There was a better view of the cabin from there, and I could see a body lyin' almost in front of the door. There was a horse saddled, but with no rider, grazin' maybe twenty yards north of the cabin. Pete was watchin' the cowboy in the corral, I was up alongside him. I reached out and touched his sleeve, and said in a whisper, "I think I can see somethin' lyin' in the grass up by that horse. That's your second man."

He nodded. "That's Waco's horse across there, that buckskin. They must have discovered the rustlers, gotten off the three shots we heard, then been cut down. After that, the rustlers figured there was no one else around, so they could take their time and choose what they wanted. They'll be movin' that whole herd into the corral, pickin' out the calves they want – you can be sure they'll take the best ones. We'll wait them out."

While we sat our horses back in the protection of the aspen, we watched as the old cows moved into the corral. They'd been through roundups all their lives, and they went right in through the gate. The calves followed along, trottin' kinda tippytoed and bein' pushed back into line once in a while by one of the cowboys. It was still a long shot from where we were in the trees to the cowboys was at the back of the herd. But I was nursin' my Winchester in the crook of my arm, and I was ready. It looked like, as Pete had said, if we could wait them out, we had a pretty good chance of taggin' the lot.

But Pete's stallion done us in. Some of those cowboys must've been ridin' mares, and the wind was driftin' our way. That stallion got the scent, and of a sudden he pricked up his ears and lurched forward two or three nervous steps. Before he could stop the damned animal, Pete got carried out into the open, away from the trees. He jerked the reins, pulled the stallion to a halt, and backed him into the trees. But the damage was done.

The rustlers in the back, who'd been pushin' the cows into the corral, were facin' right toward us, and they caught Pete's movement. The cowboy at the gate pulled his gun and fired right at Pete. I heard a bullet thud into him. I didn't think that cowboy'd seen me. I lifted my Winchester, steadied it, and squeezed off a shot. He dropped off his horse.

Pete was still on his stallion and he moved deeper into the trees. They couldn't see us now, but that didn't stop them firin' at where we'd been. When the shootin' started, the cattle began to spook, and the rustlers didn't seem sure whether to charge the location of the shots, try to round up the herd, or just to hightail it away.

Nudgin' Tempter up alongside the stallion, I looked over at Pete.

"I'm all right," he said. "Damned stallion!" Blood was comin' from below his right shoulder, stainin' his shirt, and runnin' on down his side. He didn't look all right to me.

"That wound's gonna take some care pretty quick, Pete."

"I'm all right," he insisted, "but I'd admit I'm not much good for shootin'."

I got Tempter swung around, lifted the Winchester, and took aim at the nearest rider out there. They were all still movin' slowly, lookin' as if they couldn't make up their minds what to do. That helped my aimin', but still it was a hard shot, through the trees like that. It looked like I'd maybe hit the horse. At least, she stumbled and the rider got dumped on the ground. The cowboy picked himself up and began to run, but he was wearin' chaps and he was a slow target.

I jacked another shell into the chamber and took more careful aim. He spun around and went down, but he was up again, limpin' and tryin' to run zig zag, like a jackrabbit gittin' away from a coyote. A second rustler swept in and the one I'd hit swung aboard behind him.

Their minds were made up now, and they galloped away from the corral. I pumped another shot at the two of them, but they were too far away and runnin' too fast. The third one made up his mind and he galloped off to the north behind the other two, runnin' alongside the empty horse'd dumped the first cowboy, catchin' the horse and grabbin' the reins. I'd mostly scared that horse, it seemed like, not actually hit him. They all rode off, followed by little trails of dust.

I slid my Winchester back into the boot, and was ready to follow them. But I looked over toward Pete, and he was swayin' in the saddle. I moved toward him and put my arm around him.

"Easy, friend," I said. "Let's get you over to the cabin." He was mad as hell.

"Let's chase those bastards!" he growled.

But I knew it was no good. "Better look at that shoulder first," I said. Keepin' an eye out to see there were no rustlers we'd missed, we rode over to the cabin. I helped Pete off the stallion and propped him on the ground against the logs on the front of the cabin. After I slit a hole in his shirt and took a look at where he'd been shot, I figured it wasn't all that serious, even if he'd lost a load of blood. The bullet seemed to have gone through without smashin' the shoulder.

There was a bucket of water at the corner of the cabin, and I dipped my neckerchief into it and cleaned the wound some. Pete was kinda groggy by then, but I squeezed the neckerchief out, and handed it to him.

"Hold this tight against that hole in your shoulder. It'll help stop the bleedin'. I'd better go over and check that cowboy by the gate and lift his gun. I'd hate to have him wake up and start firin' at us."

Lookin' at the cowboy lyin' there, I saw he was dead all right. But I figured not to take any chances, so I dismounted and pulled his gun, and left him there. I'd already seen that the Circle R cowboy, right by the cabin, was dead. He'd caught it full in the chest.

But I wanted to check out the other Circle R man was lyin' in the grass out where the roan horse was grazin'. It was Waco Martin, the same skinny kid had brought the message to me up to the hotel in Trevorton, the message about Ferret Watson. He was alive all right, and as I looked down on him, he tried to sit up but couldn't make it. I jumped off Tempter and examined the kid. He'd been shot some in the side, and he had a lump on his head, most likely from fallin' off the horse. He'd lost some blood from the wound, but he was goin' to make it.

"You're all right, son," I said. "I'll help you back to the cabin gentle as I can."

He opened his eyes and looked up at me, pretty confused. "You're Krieger!" he mumbled. "You know who one of those rustlers was? He's Trigger Watson. I hope you got him."

"Maybe next time," I said. "He mighta been the one I plinked in the leg, but the only one's dead is the one was at the corral. I'll just owe Watson. Let's get you back to the cabin now."

CHAPTER 12

As I rode up the grade that went into Alta Vista, I felt like I was comin' home. I never felt that way about a town before. I guess I'd been in a hundred places, and I was usually as ready to ride out as I'd been to ride in. Alta Vista was different.

The Mueller kids were comin' down the street, bent on somethin' or other. But they all stopped and shouted to me when I rode past. I waved to them.

Even Tempter acted like he was back home. I never put a hand onto steerin' him with the reins, and he trotted right smart like to the O'Malley Livery Stable. He knew where the feed was. When I got down, Mike O'Malley came up, shook my hand, and I noticed he said, "Welcome home!"

He helped me unsaddle Tempter, and I set to cleanin' up the horse out back of the stable – his dun color was pretty dusty after comin' up across the San Luis Valley from the Circle R. Lookin' up once while I worked, I saw Colleen there. I waved to her and said, "Hello, Colleen," which was as much as I could think of to say. My heart was doin' tricks, though.

She was ridin' bareback, her legs were in fringed buckskin trousers, and she was wearin' soft, beaded moccasins had to've come from Plains Indians. Mike musta bought them for her when he was in Denver sometime. Her black hair was braided Indian style and was hangin' down in front of her shoulders. Her shirt was tight on her, and I could see her breasts outlined under the shirt.

After I spoke, I was watchin' her pretty careful. She made some signal with her eyes, somethin' that said "Hello!" back to me. Then her whole face smiled at me, and then she was gone. With leg pressure and movin' the reins so little I couldn't even see her hands change, the pinto swung around and trotted back up the street.

Mike, he was standin' there watchin' me, and I felt my face go red. He musta understood some kind of message that went back and forth between Colleen and me.

"You know," I said, "you'll never make an Irish lass out of that beautiful Indian woman." It was the first time I'd spoken to O'Malley about Colleen, and I knew now I was no longer thinkin' of her as a little girl, but as a woman.

"Irish, Indian, Mexican – whatever she is," Mike said, "What we want is that she have some happiness, Krieger. I'll tell you, though, she's an independent spirit – that must be the Irish! We've tried to keep her ridin' to stay inside the town. But she goes off by herself out on the flat, in spite of that, and it makes Erla and me fearful. There're too many men hereabout that know what's happened to her, and it gives them bad ideas. They don't think of an Indian woman as a human being."

I understood what Mike meant, and it gave me an idea, but I wasn't sure if I was too shy to talk it over with Mike or not. I'd grown up without much bringin' up, mostly I had to find out on my own how to behave. And sometimes, like now, I wasn't sure how I was supposed to act – 'specially not when it came to women. I brushed Tempter a minute, then decided to get on with it.

"Mike," I began. "I'm goin' to be ridin' through the valley lookin' for farmland the next few days. Would you..." I stopped a minute, not quite sure how to put what I wanted to say. "Would you, uhh...give me permission...would you allow Colleen to ride with me sometimes?"

My voice was all funny, and it wouldn't a' surprised me any if Mike O'Malley would just have said no and walked away. But he didn't.

He looked across Tempter at me and said, "Ye've my permission, Krieger. But we'd best talk with Erla, see if she's agreeable. Erla treats Colleen like the child she never had, and ye know how women are." He laughed after he said it, and I was wonderin' whether I *did* know how women were.

Then he stood up straight and looked over serious like to me. "Krieger," he began, "the girl is Indian, and any white man shows any interest in her, he'd better know he's got lots of battles ahead. A white man takin' up with an Indian, like Chris Pollock did, back in the days of the mountain men, no one thought much about it. But now it's not a thing's very accepted – lots o' folks object to that. You understand me, Krieger?"

I knew what he was drivin' at. I'd already given thought to it. But for myself, I'd been with enough Indians that I didn't figure it was any kind of a problem for me. Maybe there'd be others took exception, but I was ready for that.

"Mike, since I was a kid I fought my own battles, and I usually had a little bit of fight left over when it was done. I know there's lots of enemies, but I've found plenty of friends, too, and I can usually tell one from the other. I live my life the way it seems to me is right. Others don't like it, they can go hang. Come to trouble like you're talkin' of, I'll be ready."

Mike grinned. "Just so ye understand, Krieger." Then he stopped for a second afore he went on. "Ye know, I've a feelin' Erla may have baked an apple pie. It might be good idea if you came by for supper tonight. Colleen's been learnin' about cookin' from watchin' Erla. And she's understandin' English even better than she did, what with Erla talkin' to her all the time, and Alice Trimble, the school teacher, workin' with her. Gittin' across to her is easier every day, and while she can't talk back to ye, her eyes have a way lettin' ye know she understands...I expect ye've noticed that, Krieger!"

Mike was right, I had.

When I was walkin' across the street to the hotel I thought over what had passed between me and Mike O'Malley. I figured he understood maybe how I was beginnin' to feel about her. Maybe he even understood better than I did, 'cause I was confused. Love never happened to me before, if that's what it was was happenin'.

The next few days weren't like any others I'd ever lived. There was a happiness and a kind of excitement that I'd just never felt. I went down to the land office and looked over plats and talked with settlers, and I rode the valley huntin' for land that might be available.

First time we went out, both the O'Malleys came along. Mike said he wanted to show me some places in the valley, but I guess what they wanted was, as I'd heard people say, to know if my intentions was honorable. The second day it was plain that Colleen could go along with me, and the O'Malleys stayed at home. I didn't know but what the rest of the town might be upset, but the O'Malleys were satisfied I wasn't up to anything bad, and I didn't give a hoot in hell what the rest of the town had to say.

When we began ridin' by ourselves, Colleen rode in line behind me, like she was a well trained squaw, and I felt pretty funny. But that didn't last more'n a few minutes. I turned in the saddle when I heard her cluck to the pinto, and then she was gone, racin' her pony off to chase antelope. Mike had bought her a beautiful silver ornamented saddle down in Denver, but she mostly left it back on the rack in the stable, and came along ridin' bareback.

The Apache Indians were always supposed to be the best riders in the world, but I'll tell you, they'd never keep up with this Ute woman called Colleen O'Malley. We had a great time. There was nothin' ever like it for me, and even if Colleen could say nothin' in words, she made it plain she was happy. I never touched her, but seemed to me we both understood there was more gonna happen between us sometime.

We really were scoutin' the valley for farmland, but it took me only a few days to know that Chris Pollock owned the finest piece of land in the whole place, and that most the rest of the land seemed to be held by the Hoovers, though their property had water troubles. I found some other settlers either ranchin' or were tryin' to farm in a little, family sort of way. But none of these came to any account. Maybe I'd set my sights too high, but I wanted a real place, not some little two by four with a garden in the backyard. I figured I'd have to spend some more time lookin', maybe even go farther from Alta Vista.

One of the days we'd ridden out, we came back past Pollock's cabin. He was up there takin' the pack off Balky. Shine, the roan he rode, was already unsaddled and loose in the corral below the cabin. We rode up to the place, and got off. Pollock shook my hand, then put his arm lightly around Colleen.

"It's my understandin'," he said to me, "that you found yourself a companion." I didn't know exactly what to say, and I settled for mumblin', "Seem to've." I was still shy talkin' about the whole thing.

"That's well and good," said Pollock, "And tell you the truth, I hate to interfere with this, but you and me'd better get to work on that claim pretty quick or you'll never make enough money to buy the land you want. Before the first real snowfall up there, we'd better use your muscles to get some work done. First thing, we're gonna build that cabin onto the front of the cave. I've already got us a little stove hauled up there. And I've already put up some lodgepole rails for a corral fence, too."

He stopped for a minute and looked over toward me. "Krieger," he continued. "you're still with me, ain't you?"

Tell you the truth, since Colleen and I'd been ridin' out lookin' for farmland, I'd not given much thought to minin'. But Pollock was right, we'd best get on with it, and I'd promised.

"You bet, Chris. I'll help you pick up the supplies tomorrow and when we're ready, we can load up Balky and Polly, and get back up there and go to work.

"Don't suppose you've found no land in the valley you liked?" he asked me.

"Not yet," I admitted. "But I guess there'll still be some lookin' to be done." When I glanced over at Colleen, I knew she understood our days of ridin' together were over for now. We'd both miss them, all right, but there'd be other times, I'd see to that.

One of the things I can't abide is loud mouths. I learned a long time back that they come in all kinds of faces, and the faces are attached to short bodies, tall bodies, thin and fat ones. In the towns I'd been livin' in, loud mouths tended to be young 'cause as they got older they either changed their ways or they annoyed someone with a touchy trigger finger. I look on myself as a peaceable man unless there's some cause to be otherwise, and I've always figured anyone had a right to speak up pretty much however they wanted to. But like most things, there's limits, and I come up against the limit in the Mother Lode Café that night.

Doc Train and I had agreed to have supper there, and when I found Pollock was in town, he said he'd join up with us. He'd been buyin' the last supplies at the Weintraub's store for us to take up in the mornin'. We'd all had a drink and the waitress took our order for supper when I heard a loud voice just a few feet back o' me at the bar. That cowboy had had enough liquor to make his voice loud, but his words weren't messed up none. What he said was clear enough that everyone heard it.

When I finally stood up and walked over to where he was, I saw he was younger than me, sandy haired, and he had a thickness about the middle that comes from too much drinkin' and too little work. When I'd first heard him I wasn't sure whether he was talkin' to someone else at the bar, or whether he meant for the whole room to hear.

"I slept with a lotta Indian women," he'd been sayin'. "From here clear back to St. Louis. I must have enough half breed kids by now to start up a tribe o' my own. But I tell you, I've never seen no Indian whore as pretty as that one rides the pinto here in town. Whoooeeee! I gotta…"

But that was as far as he got. I'd shoved my chair back and moved across to the bar, mostly all in one movement. I grabbed the cowboy by the shoulders, spun him around, and I think my fist, as it hit his jaw, was louder than his talk had been. I let him go and he slumped down onto the floor. I looked to the cowboys on either side of where he'd been standin'. They were interested, all right, but it was plain they weren't reachin' for their guns.

"Johnny," I said to the bartender, "you got some soap back there?"

He looked a little wide eyed. "Yessir."

"Good, dark brown lye soap?"

"Yessir, I think so."

"Got some hot water back on the stove in the kitchen?"

He understood now. "Yessir, Mr. Krieger."

"Shave a chunk of that lye soap into a pan of that hot water, melt it down and let it boil away a minute or two."

Johnny disappeared into the kitchen. By this time the cowboy on the floor sat up, and he was feelin' his jaw.

"Just keep that gun hand up there on your jaw," I advised him. "If you reach for that revolver, I'll kill you."

"What the hell's the matter with you?" he asked. "Everybody knows that Indian girl shacked up with the Watsons, and from what I hear she most likely shot those two men she was found with. She' nothin' but a..."

He was still sittin' on the floor, and the best I could do was to let fly with a boot. I caught him in the stomach, knocked the wind outta him, and I figured his ribs would take a few days to get back in place. He gasped for air, but he never touched his gun or I would have killed him. By now Johnny was back with a tumbler of steamin' soapy water. It was an awful brownish green color and a couple of chunks of soap were still floatin' in it.

"Mister," I said, "I don't know who in hell you are, but we don't talk about women, includin' Indian women, like that around here. Now, you wash your mouth out some." I put the tumbler on the floor in front of him.

"Drink that," I said. "All of it."

"I ain't..." he started. But I wasn't in any mood to put up with backtalk.

"Yes, you are..." I told him. "Every drop of it." I shifted my foot, ready to kick him again. He reached for the glass, put it to his lips, and took several quick swallows, makin' an awful face.

"All of it!" I shouted. "Every damn drop."

He drained the glass, and was chewin' away on the pieces of soap.

"Now, git outside," I told him. "I've a feelin' you're gonna need to settle your stomach some. Don't come back while I'm here, and don't ever talk like that about women again."

The man ran for the door and the whole room could hear him begin to throw up as he lurched onto the sidewalk. I took a look around at the rest of the cowboys at the bar, said "Thanks, Johnny" to the bartender, and walked back to our table. Only when I sat down this time, I changed my place so I'd be facin' the door if trouble walked through it.

"I guess you know that's goin' to be a pretty sick cowboy," Doc said. "If you've brought me another patient, Krieger, I'm goin' to be unhappy. He' didn't look like he'd have the money for an office call."

"Well," said Pollock. "One thing, he'll sure have clean intestines. You be ready to load up first thing in the mornin', Krieger?"

"I'll be ready," I said.

When I caught up with him, Pollock was already waterin' his stock a few feet off the trail. I got down and led Tempter to the edge of the pond, and I pulled on Polly's lead rope so she came along to the water, too. I took a breath of the fall air, and looked over across the beaver pond. It was really a sight to see, and there's no place but the Rockies like that in the fall. Those hard, sharp, treeless peaks – they were still way higher'n where we stood. They were covered with new snow that glistened in the sun, and the white reached down into tree line. Just opposite where we were, a grove of aspen made the whole mountainside a shimmerin' sparklin' yellow. This whole thing was reflected in the water that had been rippled only by Tempter and Polly drinkin'.

"It's sights like these," Chris said quietly to me, "that've kept me livin' in the mountains these many years." We checked our packs, mounted up, and rode on up to the mine.

Just below timberline there was an inch or two of last night's snow in the woods, but by the time we got up to the valley that had our cave in it, most of the snow was melted off. On the peaks, though, up the steep granite walls above us, the snow was a lot deeper, and Chris said he thought that upper snow might be there the whole winter.

"If we keep gettin' these warm days, though, that'll help our stream flow and sluicin'll be easier."

"That's right," I agreed, "but before we get to minin' we'd best work for ourselves. Soon's we're unpacked we'll start on buildin' the log front for the cave."

"I'd guess it'll take us most of a week," Chris said. "'cause if we're gonna do it, it's got to be strong enough that the avalanches'll just slide down over it. I don't aim to rebuild it next summer. If we put in hefty logs, 'n reinforce them every way, I doubt we'll have more trouble. But Krieger, I got no intention o' stayin' up here to find out about the avalanches. I'm gonna be safely down in Vista in that cabin o' mine."

It was hard work, cuttin' and notchin' the logs, and draggin' them up to the cave. On account of the cave was twenty feet off the valley floor, and 'cause the trail to it was too narrow for a horse, I rigged up a log supported pulley against the roof of the cave, and that let us snake logs up the cliffside, usin' Balky for power. Chris, he stayed below and managed the mule. I worked up on the floor of the cave, handlin' the logs as they came up. Even with this help it took us a week before we got the cave finished up.

But when it was done we had us a snug cabin, with a door that opened onto the path down to the valley floor, a window that gave us some light, along with a little view of the valley, and the tiny potbelly stove that heated the place and had cookin' space on top. The cave slanted down toward the back, so we had lots of storage room for our gear, where we could leave stuff safely all winter, out of the snow.

Pollock thought the cabin was a fine place, all right, but he was impatient. "Let's get on with the minin'," he argued. But we were partners, and I had my ideas about minin', too.

"Chris, you've been workin' the placer in the creek. Lookin' at your cleanup, that gold's good – there's a lot of heavier stuff in with the color. But you were right the other day, somewhere up above here there's hardrock, and you can bet if we find the right place, you'll find more gold there than you'll get outta that creek in the next ten years. If you agree, you go ahead with the rocker, I'm goin' to poke around up above, maybe climb some walls. Even if we don't get to any of the quartz this fall, if we can locate high pay up there, we'll be in shape to get at it in a bigger way come next spring."

We'd carried up a supply of dynamite and had stored it carefully in the farthest back section of the cave. I took some of this along with me when I began diggin' up above. By the time I'd put in a couple of days, I'd found several veins looked promisin', and one I thought was special worth workin' more. Chris came up to help, and we began a tunnel straight across into the rock.

He went back to the creek after a while, leavin' me up there, and I put in a week workin' with a pick, a drill, and when I needed it, a little blast of the dynamite. By that time I was satisfied we were into a productive vein. It maybe wasn't the best outcroppin' on the mountain, and it wasn't anythin' like the lode I'd found at San Badillo. But still it would be enough to keep us workin', and after maybe part of a summer's work I'd most likely have found enough to get started on a farm. I was countin' on findin' a place suited me, but so far I had to admit Pollock's place was the only one I'd want.

It was getting' on into late fall now, but there'd been no fresh snow as low as our diggin's, though once in a while the afternoon storms would whiten the peaks above us. We were getting' kinda low on grub and supplies, and as we sat in the cabin one night, we decided we'd both go down the mountain. If we got a good snow, Chris argued, we might be stuck a couple weeks, and we'd be pretty hungry after a bit. We could always shoot a deer, but a little flour and little syrup would taste good.

"Maybe you kin talk Erla O'Malley into lettin' you bring back one o' her apple pies," Chris said. "Krieger, you know you got both those ladies charmed. You never asked my opinion," he added, "but you know that Indian girl'd make you a good wife. You and her'd get along. Maybe she cant' talk, but there's more to bein' married than jus' talkin'. 'Specially at your age. I think we'd better get back down that valley and look after matters."

I looked across at him by the light of the lamp we had hangin' up by the ceilin', and he was grinnin' away. I didn't disagree with him. Fact is, I had Tempter saddled and Polly's pack on before dawn. Chris came along behind, grumblin' about havin' to get up so early. We took the pack animals on out to Chris' corral, and came back into town and went over to the assay office to turn in the gold we'd brought down from the cleanup.

Runnin' into Doc on the street, we agreed to have supper with him, then Chris went on to Weintraub's, and I rode Tempter back to O'Malley's stable. Colleen was there, along with both Erla and Mike. She and Erla were wearin' dresses, and although Colleen's black hair was still done in that Indian way, I felt today she was lookin' more Irish than Indian. But one or the other, she was more beautiful even than I'd remembered, and I felt myself gettin' red up from my collar.

Erla O'Malley invited me to dinner, but I'd already promised Doc and Chris. I told her, though, I'd be in town tomorrow night, too, and maybe I was a mite eager.

"We'll expect you then," she laughed at me, and I was pretty embarrassed. When I looked over at Colleen she was smilin' at me, pretty as could be.

When I came into the Mother Lode, Doc was sittin' back at his usual table. Some of the Hoover cowboys were in at the bar, and they were still drinkin' when we got up to leave. As we stood there by the door, Chris said, "Krieger, I'll meet you back up at the mine. I figure I kin get Balky loaded and be out of here early. I'll be back up there workin' before the end of the afternoon. If the extra dynamite comes in, you'll likely be up day after tomorrow. Way things'r goin', guess you wouldn't mind an extra day down here now, would ya?"

I never paid any mind to the cowboys in the bar, but later, after what happened, I was sure that's how they'd known, and I should have been more worried about Chris. But I couldn't see that then, and it does no good to look back after it's all over.

CHAPTER 13

When I rode back past the corral up at the mine, both of Chris' animals were in the corral. I unloaded Polly and Tempter at the end of the walk above the cave, then carried most of the supplies, including the dynamite, up along the walk, and stored them in the back of the cave.

There was somethin' peculiar, and it hadn't struck me right off, but it kinda stayed in my mind waitin' for attention. There'd been a light dustin' of snow up here, and I figured it had to be from the night before. When I walked up to the cabin there were no footprints on the ledge. If that snow'd come down durin' the night, then Chris hadn't slept in the cabin.

There wasn't anything to be alarmed about, not yet. But I figured I'd better look into it. I picked up some of the supplies that was to go up to the mine, and I left the horses tied at the foot of the walk. Chris most likely was up at the rocker or maybe he'd be diggin' away up at the mine tunnel.

But something kept gnawin' away at my mind that was makin' me uneasy.

He wasn't at the rocker, so I hurried on toward the tunnel. When I looked up from the valley floor, I saw we had real trouble, real big trouble. Even from down there I could see the timbers at the entrance were knocked down, and the openin' was almost blocked by rubble.

I dropped the stuff I was carryin' and raced up the trail to the entrance. The timbers were all splintered, and up here I saw the rubble was hip high. The only thing I could figure, a blast must have gone off in the wrong place. But somethin' told me right away that didn't make sense. We'd been blastin' little tiny shots at a face maybe ten feet back into the wall. This had been a bigger blast, and it had to've been right out here by the entrance.

Where the hell was Chris? I didn't like the looks of any of it. I stood there a few seconds, tryin' to fathom it out, and then I saw the boots, toes down, stickin' out of the rubble on the mine floor. Chris had to be in those boots. I tore at the rocks with my bare hands, and pushed all that junk aside. I knew that whoever it was, he was long since dead, but somethin' inside me kept sayin' maybe I was wrong and he'd be all right. My hands were scraped to bleedin', but it took me only a few minutes until I pulled the body out of the rubble.

It was Chris, of course. While I'd been diggin' I'd been thinkin' about how all this could've happened, and I'd about convinced myself that Chris'd been carryin' dynamite back into the mine, and then somehow it'd set itself off and brought down the whole entrance on top of him.

When I looked at Chris lyin' there, though, I knew it wasn't that way. He'd been face down when I pulled him out, and the back of his coat was ripped and looked like it might have been burned some. It wasn't torn apart, though. I dreaded doin' it, but I rolled him over. There was a bloody wound across his chest that'd dried long since. That seemed to make sense if the blast went off in front of him.

It did at first look, but not for long. If he'd been standin' in the entrance, and that blast went off strong enough to bring down timbers and all that rock, the concussion would just have blown him on out of the mine and over the edge. At the least, his clothes would have been tore off him. But it was the back of his coat was messed up.

It didn't all fit together, no way I figured it. But what little sense I could make, I didn't like. It was only when I began to think of other ways it might have been that anything started to make real sense. And all those other ways seemed to say that Chris had been murdered.

Whatever it was, it was a lot to figure out, and I sat down on the rubble, out by the entrance. Chris' body was only a few feet from me, stretched out on the floor. The afternoon sun was on his face, makin' him look haunted like.

If there bein' no footprints in the snow at the cave was right, whatever happened, it happened yesterday. I was still sittin' there, tryin' to puzzle it all out, and I must have seen the stain on the rock for several seconds before it stuck in my mind. It was there on the ledge where we'd cut the trail up the rock face. No rubble'd been blown that far. It was a dark red stain, and I could see it on several rocks along there. It had to be blood.

Walkin' over to it, I knelt down and looked at it careful. It had long since dried.

If it was Chris' blood, then how could the blast have splattered it out that far? Guess I think pretty slow, or maybe I was fightin' what this all meant. But the only way I could figure it was that Chris' body, already bleedin', had been brought in here to the mine, and then maybe the blast had been set off, after.

If he'd been lyin' face down when the dynamite went, that would account for the back of his coat bein' burned. I walked across and looked down at Chris again. Inside his chest, where all the blood was, there had to be a bullet. He just had to have been shot somewhere else and brought here. That's the only way it all fit together.

Chris never wore a gun when he worked the claim, nor even kept a rifle handy. If he'd been shot, it was in cold blood. I went over and sat down again on the rubble. I had to think this through. I looked down the valley to the rocker, and up to the cabin on the west wall. In a few minutes the sun would go off the gulch here. I got up and walked down the ramp.

I knew what I was lookin' for – blood. And I found it, several places there were smears of blood on the rocks. I was hopin' I'd find a footprint, though I'd already messed up the trail along here myself. But on the ramp the stones were too big, and there was too little dust for prints. But when I walked down toward the rocker, I found part of the rest of the puzzle.

The sand down here was finer, and it kept images better'n up on the ramp. Here and there a pair of cowboy boots had left prints goin' up the ramp, and had come back down, too. I put my own boot alongside one of the prints comin' away from the mine. The boot was close to my size, and I noticed right away how the heel, it was the left boot, had a big slash down through it, where it must've got cut on somethin'. It looked almost as if a knife had sliced along the heel, but the cut was wider'n that. Still thinkin', tryin' to figure it out, I walked back up the ramp and took a look at Chris' boots. That print was never made by his boots, and I knew it didn't match mine.

So far, the way I figured it, Chris had been shot somewhere down below, then got carried or dragged up there. When I went back down to the rocker, I found where he'd been shot, all right. There was a large patch of bloody sand there. I could only figure that whoever killed him had wanted to hide how he'd died, make it seem accidental. They'd not done a very smart job of it.

Robbin' a claim wasn't unknown. I looked down into the rocker. It hadn't been cleaned out. There wasn't much collection of color in it, but enough that if Chris had been killed to rob the claim, they'd have taken time to clean out the rocker.

If the way I figured it was right, then there shouldn't be any blood beyond the rocker. I walked on down the trail and looked careful as I could, but I was right, there was no more blood. I went down almost as far as the cabin. Whoever came in must have come up on foot first, maybe clear up from the corral so that if Pollock was workin' up there, he'd never even have heard their horses. And it seemed most likely that whoever did the shootin' did it from as far away as he could.

Walkin' on down to the corral, I looked around. I'd not noticed when I'd come up from town with Tempter and

Polly, but I wasn't lookin' for anything then. On the far corner of the outside of the corral, horses'd been tethered on the corral rail. I walked back up the trail, figurin' I was carryin' a rifle and tryin' to find where I'd come into sight of Pollock if he was workin' at the rocker. I walked up until I could see the rocker, then I stopped and looked around, but there was no sign of any sort of upset there. Then, I got to thinkin' how it would've looked up there at the rocker. Pollock would've been standin' up, and a man comin' up the way I just did, he'd a seen Pollock much quicker than he saw the rocker. Pollock woulda been maybe three or four feet higher than the top of the rocker.

Walkin' back down a ways, I found the place all right. There was a big boulder about five feet off the trail. The sun was gone now, and it was getting' dark, but I thought I could make out where someone had walked cross to the boulder, and when I looked careful I could see boot prints at the base of the rock.

There was somethin' else, too, and that's what I wanted. I picked up the cartridge. It was a Henry '44. Chris had to've been killed from down here, probably with the shooter leanin' on the big rock. Chris'd never even known he was there. It was pure cold blooded murder, thought out ahead of time. That son of a bitch.

Whoever shot him might've fired twice, and left the second cartridge in the chamber. But at that distance, with a Henry, a single shot in the chest, like Chris had, was plenty to kill. I jammed the shell into my pocket, and walked over to the corral.

Polly and Tempter were still tied there, and Polly had her empty packsaddle on yet. I wanted to get Chris back down to town, and I decided I'd leave his animals up at the mine. They had enough grass in the corral to hold them a few days, and the stream in the corner wasn't froze solid yet. I was dreadin' what I had to do.

Tyin' the horses to some brush at the foot of the ramp at the mine, I walked up to where Chris was, carryin' a canvas pack cover. Gentle as I could, I wrapped Chris in the canvas, tied it, and carried it back down and lashed it to the packsaddle on Polly. Polly, I don't know whether she could smell the blood, but she sidestepped and I swore at her and jerked her back.

It was gonna be a long night. I stopped and tied up the horses when I got back down by the cabin. I went inside and lit a lamp, found some jerky and handful of biscuits, and took a long drink of water from a bucket Chris'd brought up.

That poor old man. He'd been kinder to me than anyone I'd ever known, except maybe Maria and Juan. And now he was out there, his body trussed up in canvas, loaded on a packhorse. I'd find out who did it. Fact is, I was already pretty sure I knew the answer.

By the time I mounted up, the stars were out and a half moon threw enough light to help with the trail. It wasn't a ride I enjoyed. Not one bit.

If whoever murdered Pollock was along the trail, I figured I'd most likely be dead by mornin'. But I was bettin' whoever did it was already back in town. Either they went back right after they killed Pollock and dragged his body up to the mine, or they'd ridden down today, and somehow managed not to meet me as I came up.

The thing is, they just had to've known that Pollock was comin' back up to the mine by himself, and that I wasn't comin' up 'til later. I remembered then our discussin' it as we were leavin' the Mother Lode, and Hoover's cowboys sittin' there at the bar. As I rode down through the lodgepole, I was thinkin' of Hoover's threat to Chris Pollock, and it just seemed natural to me it was Hoover, one way or another, made good on that threat.

By the time I rode into town, I could look out to the east and see mornin' comin' on. It'd been a long night, and I was mighty tired and low as I rode up Main Street toward Doc Train's. I pounded on the door. No one else in town seemed awake yet. I pounded again, and after a while a light appeared in the back of the house, and I saw Doc movin' up the hallway carryin' a lamp. He looked out through the door pretty careful before he opened up.

"For God's sake," he said. "What're you doin' down here? I thought you went up to the mine yesterday."

"Doc," I said, "when I got there Pollock had been shot."

"Shot!" He held the lamp up a little, took a good look at me. "Krieger, you look like you need a drink. Come on in back."

I needed the drink, all right, but I said, "Doc, first I have him out here. Don't seem right just to leave him there on Polly, all trussed up in a piece of canvas. Can we bring him in?"

He looked out, and he could see the bundle on Polly. "God damn it," he said. "That poor old man."

We unlashed the bundle off Polly and carried Chris into Doc's office, still wrapped in canvas, and put him onto one of those long tables doctors always have in their offices.

"I'll examine him later," said Doc, then he put his hand on my shoulder. "Why don't you have that drink? You can tell me what happened up there."

When I'd finished my story, I added, "I know right now there's no evidence, Doc, but it's got to have been Hoover's men did this. No claim jumper or ordinary thief would have taken the trouble to try to hide the murder."

Doc told me I'd likely have to repeat my story because the sheriff would want to know how Pollock died. "But I'll tell you," he added, "if the sheriff suspects Hoover, he's not going to do anything. Ben Little may be sheriff, but I'd put him down as one of Hoover's men, too. If I were you, Krieger, I'd skip that part about finding the cartridge, and the heel print. You tell Ben that, and there's going to be a Henry rifle and a pair of boots in the ground ten minutes later. Let's just keep that to ourselves, and there's at least some chance we'll end up knowin' who was there.

"After he hears your story, Ben's probably going to insist we find out for sure Pollock was really shot. He'd rather believe a blast of dynamite went off accidentally. I'll have to find the bullet – I'm the nearest thing to a coroner there is up here in Alta Vista. From what you've said, it didn't go clean through him, and finding it won't be much of a job."

"Doc," I said, "it just isn't right, an old man like that killed because he owned a chunk of land somebody wanted to have."

He looked at me kind of funny. "Did Pollock ever talk to you about what would become of that farm when he died? Or his share of the mine?"

"No, Doc," I said. "Far as I know he hadn't any kin. He never mentioned any – the Cheyenne woman he lived with died a long time back, he told me."

"He had no kin," Doc said. "But after we bury him, you'd best come over to the lawyer's office. You'd better be there when he talks about the mine, since you already own half of it."

What with the whiskey, I was beginnin' to feel pretty bleary eyed, and Doc saw it. "Look," he said, "you've been runnin' for twenty four hours, maybe longer. Why don't you go over to the hotel and get some sleep. I'll get hold of the sheriff and he'll be over there along about noon."

"Hell, Doc," I said, "I don't know whether I can go to sleep with Chris lyin' in there on the table, dead." But when I got over to the Senate, I had no trouble sleepin'. I was wore out, all right.

When I woke up there was a note on the door sayin' I should come on over to the sheriff's office. Ben Little was a nervous, skinny, unimportant sort of man you see in bars, drinkin' in the corner alone. He got his job, I figured, because no one else would take it. He was lookin' for as little trouble as possible, and from what I'd heard he'd knuckle under to anyone shouted loud enough. He wasn't much of a sheriff, but until now at least, Alta Vista hadn't asked a lot of him.

Like Doc suggested, when I talked to Ben I said nothin' about findin' the shell or about the heel print, and when I'd finished, he said, "Doc Train found the bullet in Pollock's chest when he operated this morning. It was murder all right."

Then he looked across right at me. "And Doc said Pollock had to have been dead before you ever left town yesterday morning. That says you couldn't have shot him."

Tell you the truth, that had never even come to my mind. But now it was in the open I could see this might have been a possibility to the sheriff. After all, Pollock and I'd been partners. Doc had solved that, it looked like.

"You got any ideas who might have done this, Krieger? You knew the old man better than most folks here."

I thought that one over for a few seconds. "He didn't have any enemies I know of," I said. "Though Hoover wanted his land the worst kind of way."

I watched the sheriff pretty careful after I dropped that, but he just looked blank, as if I'd never said anything.

"From what I could see up there," I went on, "whoever did it took the trouble to try to hide it was murder, even if they messed it up." I paused a couple of seconds, then went on. "I think you ought to go back up there with me, sheriff. I've got to bring the two animals of Pollock's back here before they get snowed in. You might find somethin' up there I didn't know to look for. It was almost dark when I had a chance to hunt around."

But Ben Little wasn't about to buy that. "Don't think that'll do much for us, Krieger. Lookin' up at the mountains this mornin', I guess there must be at least a foot of snow up there in that valley. Anything's there, it's likely to stay 'til spring now. I doubt we'll ever know who killed Pollock, or why."

So that was that. When I walked out of the office I was wonderin' whether he'd have had any interest if I'd told him about the cartridge and the heel print. I doubted it, and likely Doc was right. A pair of boots and a Henry rifle would have disappeared mighty quick. I suspected that Ben Little might already know who killed Chris Pollock, and he intended to do the least possible about findin' the guilty party.

Me, I knew who had to be behind it. Provin' that might be somethin' else. But I was goin' to try.

We had no regular buryin' ground in Alta Vista yet, and it was Erla O'Malley felt Chris would like to be buried on his own place. There were long shadows across the aspen grove on the ridge back o' the cabin as we took the wooden box from the wagon. There were maybe ten of us there, standin' on the hilltop, and it was Hans Mueller, wearin' a black suit and a black tie, who read the service. The wind blew the pages from the Bible he read from, and by the time he was finished, we most of us had tears in our eyes. I looked across at Colleen and she was cryin' good.

He finished up with that part I'd remembered hearin' at my folks' funeral:

And we commit his body to the ground, earth to earth, ashes to ashes, dust to dust, in the sure and certain hope of the

Resurrection to Eternal Life through Jesus Christ our Lord, Amen.

As he finished readin' that, we lowered the box into the ground.

When we were walkin' back down to the corral, Erla and Colleen were walkin' on ahead of Mike O'Malley and me. We'd stayed on a minute to shovel a little dirt over the coffin, and I figured to come back later with Hans Mueller and finish fillin' up the grave.

Lawyer Miller, who'd been up on the hill with us, was waitin' by his horse. He said quietly to me and to Mike, "Can you both be in my office tomorrow morning? Mike, you'd best bring the Missus and the girl."

I'd been goin' to ride up to the mine to get Pollock's two animals and bring them down, but this sounded important, so I figured if I was lucky it wouldn't snow for another day, and those animals could make out up there another day yet.

We agreed to be there, and the lawyer rode off to town. I had supper with the O'Malleys and Colleen. It was a kind of sad evenin', but better than sittin' alone in the hotel after fillin' up Chris Pollock's' grave.

Lawyer Miller showed us to chairs in his small office. There was Doc Train, Erla and Mike O'Malley, Colleen and me. I was surprised when Doc showed up, and I wondered what was goin' to come of this.

After we were all sittin' down, the lawyer went back over to his desk. I'd have to give it to him. I think there were more books around his office than even Doc Train had. But all the lawyer's books seemed to look about the same.

"We were sorry to hear of Mr. Pollock's death," he began. "He was a kind man, and as you will see, maybe even kinder than you knew. To have been murdered was indeed an unfair fate, and I hope the criminal will be found and brought to justice."

Already, I was getting' kind of rutchy in my chair, and all those words didn't help much. He reminded me of one time in Kansas City, I'd gone to a play with some trail hands. It was in a theatre with gas light, and there was lots of paint on the actors' faces, and everythin' they said seemed twice as big as life. That's what Lawyer Miller sounded like, one of them actors. And we were the audience for his actin'.

He cleared his throat and went on. "Earlier this summer I saw Mr. Pollock professionally for the first time since I'd arranged the papers for the purchase of his land. I drew up the agreement you signed, Mr. Krieger, making you partners with Mr. Pollock in the mine. I saw him only once more. Three weeks ago, it was September the third to be exact..." He took time to fix his glasses up on his nose and to look down at some stuff was on his desk.

"Christian Pollock came into this office and told me he wanted me to draw up a will for him. Said he was getting on and he owned some things, and he needed to be certain what would happen to them. When I had put his wishes on paper in legal terms, he insisted that Doctor Train come to my office with him, read what the will said, and sign it as a witness. Is that correct, Doctor Train?" Doc nodded.

"He swore Doctor Train to secrecy, and of course as Mr. Pollock's lawyer, I would never have revealed any of the contents of the will. Let me now read you the essentials – I'll leave out the technical parts that aren't important:

I, Christian Pollock, being of sound mind, state that I have no known relatives presently living and therefore, at my death I wish to dispose of my holdings as follows:

My half of the mining claim I own jointly with Kurt Krieger, I give to the girl known as Colleen O'Malley, the Indian girl being raised by Mr. and Mrs. Mike O'Malley, presently of Alta Vista. Having been married to a Cheyenne woman for many years of my life, and having no children from that marriage, I would like the Indian girl, Colleen O'Malley, to have the money from whatever my share of the profits of the mine should be. For the next four years, by which time she will be approximately twenty-one, her guardian, Mr. Mike O'Malley, is empowered to make decisions for her in her best interest concerning the mine and its operation.

My land northeast of Alta Vista I wish to be given to my friend, Kurt Krieger, who presently lives in the Senate Hotel in Alta Vista.

The lawyer finished up, "Well, that's really what the will says, with a lot of added legal terms and descriptions. There you are. Mr. Krieger, you own the farmland and the cabin. And Miss O'Malley, you own Mr. Pollock's share of the mining claim."

I was pretty broke up. Doc Train was sittin' alongside me, and I turned to him. "If I could only have told him, Doc," I said, and I have to admit I was cryin' some. "The kindness of that old man...and then him bein' murdered like that..."

Doc Train, he put his hand on my shoulder, and I knew he understood how I felt.

CHAPTER 14

Tempter's hoofs sometimes stirred up a brilliant yellow splash of light as they turned up the aspen leaves that covered our trail up to Sunshine Pass. I was ridin' easy, in no hurry, and thankful for the time to be alone. It hadn't snowed up here any more, and I figured it would be easy enough to get up to the mine and back, bringin' down Chris' mule and the roan, in a day's ride.

But I'd tied on my beddin' roll and stuffed some food into the saddle bags, and thought maybe I'd stay a night or two up there. I needed some time to think over everythin' that'd happened to me the past few days. Findin' Chris Pollock dead had been pretty upsettin', and now here I was ownin' the farm, and in partnership with Colleen at the mine. It was about too much for me to take it all in.

I had to think of all the responsibilities that were pilin' up on me. Since I'd been a young kid there'd been little more to my life than just takin' the pleasures that came, and solvin' the problems one by one. Lookin' back on it, I'd enjoyed havin' the freedom of a trail hand on the move, and of crossin' the prairies, and of workin' a mine all alone. They was all just fine, but sometime back I knew that livin' like that wasn't goin' to be enough.

Now I figured I was ready for somethin' more. I'd been workin' toward that – ownin' a farm. And Pollock's dyin' had made this come true, and his place was better'n any farm I could imagine findin'. And now it looked as if Colleen and me – well, she was certainly part of any plan I was goin' to have.

But I'd never been in love before and I wasn't quite sure of how to go about it. That would work itself out, I figured, 'specially now that I already had the land and the cabin.

I'd been up along this trail often enough that I knew it well. I was ridin' through that area that had been a grove of aspen. But most of it had been cut down by beavers that had a lodge in the pond off just south of me. It was only the biggest trees was still standin'. Those beaver were smart enough they didn't tackle trees was too big for them. But I was really payin' little attention to what was around me. Truth is, I was thinkin' of Colleen.

But it mighta done me better to pay more heed, for of a sudden a bullet came in toward me, and it thunked into one of those big aspens. Seemed like it was just over my head and a little in front of me. The sound of the rifle didn't come 'til after I'd already heard the bullet hit aspen. By that time I'd dug my heels into Tempter, and he was goin' up the trail at a full gallop. I heard the second shot, but I didn't know where the bullet'd gone. I pushed Tempter on to a spruce grove that was less than a hundred feet up ahead. Once we were in there, I felt safer. I talked to Tempter a minute to settle him down, pulled my Winchester from the boot, and dismounted.

Wasn't any question those bullets were meant for me. Best I could figure, they'd come in from the north. Keepin' to the shadows in the spruces, I looked out across the edge of the clearin'. There was a tiny wisp of smoke out there, showin' up against the green of the trees, and while I watched, the smoke drifted downslope to the east. The rifleman had to be somewhere west of that smoke.

For a minute I thought of just mountin' Tempter and goin' on up the mountain to the mine. I wasn't in any mood for a gunfight, and I figured whoever shot at me probably didn't have the guts to follow me up the trail, now that I was alerted. But I guess my curiosity was too great, and I felt I had to know who had me tagged for dyin'. Besides that, I'm peaceable enough, but I've never been one to run from trouble.

Those two shots had been from a heavy gun, and I thought right off about the Henry that'd killed Chris Pollock. I was still carryin' the empty cartridge in my pocket to remind me. I kept my eye out for anything that moved, west of where the smoke had been, but I saw nothin'. Walkin' back to Tempter, I loosened the flap on the saddlebag and felt inside. I pulled out a pair of soft moccasins, took off my boots, and slipped the moccasins on. I'd nothin' against boots, but when I'd lived with the Cheyenne, I'd found moccasins were a lot quieter and made you more sure footed, and right now I needed both. Grabbin' my

Winchester, I said quietly to Tempter, "I'll be back, boy."

Somewhere up there was my enemy. I looked the ground over careful and still saw nothing. That might be good, I figured, for he likely couldn't find me either. Up toward where the smoke had been, there was a kind of openin' where the Sunshine Pass trail crossed, and north of that there was a sort of fringe of spruces. Beyond that there were a lot of young aspen, comin' up where a rock slide had knocked down the spruce forest, maybe fifty or a hundred years back. Those old dead logs were still solid, even that old, and it would be almost impossible to work my way through them. I'd have to find some way to get to the trees and the higher ground beyond the rockslide.

It made sense that the rifleman wasn't alone, even though the bullets both seemed by the sound of them to've come from the same rifle, and the time between them was enough for a gun like a Henry to be pumped. But it just seemed unlikely that whoever was after me would be by himself. I'd have to go ahead up there, thinkin' there might be more'n one person.

'Course, I thought right away of my havin' been waylaid by Tinker Barclay, and my killin' him, then bein' brought down by Ferret Watson. Getting' shot like that wouldn't happen to me again.

Off to the west side of the rock slide there was a stream with water bouncin' down through the rocks. There was alder and aspen alongside the banks, and I figured if I walked carefully up the stream I might get to the bigger trees up above, and still keep sheltered by the bank – no one in the forest up there would be able to see me.

Long ago, out on the prairies, I'd found that Indians view time different from the white man. An Indian would likely just have waited where I was, knowin' that whoever was after him would sometime be curious enough to move down the trail, to learn what'd happened. But I was a white man, and I wasn't that patient. I was goin' to move on up there and find out who it was was there.

Carryin' my Winchester in my hand, I set out up along the creek, hunched over low, walkin' fast but quiet. I worked my way along the edge of the slide below the woods, but found the bank too steep to get up, so I went farther along, maybe another seventy five feet. The rock slide here came clear to the bank o' the stream.

Slingin' my rifle onto my back now, I took a chance and worked my way up over the rocks. I tried to stay closest to those near the aspen, so I'd stay out of sight of anyone over the hump of the ridge. Once I got up there I was able to look down into the spruce thicket below me. I just lay there along the rocks, scannin' the trees, showin' myself as little as possible. I figured the rifleman had to've been there, but 'course the time it took me to move up the creek, he mighta gone on and I was still wonderin' how many there were.

For a second I got a glimpse of somethin' metallic caught the sun. It was maybe a hundred and fifty feet below me. As I kept lookin', I could gradually make out the shape of a horse, and even though the branches hid him well, I was sure that horse had a rider. Someone was still there. I unslung my Winchester, and worked my way down the slope, keepin' my eyes where I'd seen the horse. I had to be careful to keep quiet, and every time I took a step before I put my weight down, I moved my moccasin to see I was on a solid rock.

There wasn't any sign of anyone else, other'n the horse and rider – if there was a rider. When I moved in I'd have to take my chances he was alone. As I dropped down lower, I could make out the rider all right. Although I was yet a distance off, I thought it was a face I'd never seen before. He sat his roan heavy, and he kept watchin' the forest, lookin' down through the tangle of flattened spruce toward the trail. I moved my eyes along down below but could see nothin' there.

He'd swung around now, and was lookin' more away from me, and I decided I'd chance movin' in closer. His rifle was in the boot, but he had some sort of revolver in a gun belt. I was close enough now I could see him clearly, but I needed one more step to get around a tree between me and him.

That was my mistake. A branch snapped underneath my foot. The horseman wheeled, reached for his revolver, but I swung up the Winchester with one hand and fired from low down, a chance shot. Before he could clear his gun the force of the Winchester slug knocked him backward just as his horse, scared by the roar o' my gun, leaped forward.

The man hit the ground hard, his revolver still in his hand. He rolled into a flat position, and fired a single shot at me. But now I had the Winchester full up to my shoulder, and I stopped the fight. When I checked later on, I found my second shot went in through his arm, and it must've exploded in his heart.

I stayed where I was for a few seconds, lookin' for any kind of movement that would show me there was someone else. Then I heard the hoofs of a horse at the gallop. It had to be along the trail. That was the only place open enough to ride a horse that fast. The sound was faint, but there was no question the horse was headed back down toward Alta Vista. That rider'd likely been searchin' for me, but when he heard the shot he'd left his partner up here, and was runnin' for town.

There was nothin' very distinctive about the man on the ground. I'd seen he was heavyset, he had a couple days' growth of beard, and he had a long, bushy mustache. He was no one I ever knew, and he was probably a hired gun who'd drifted into Alta Vista on his way from one killin' to another.

His horse had moved on down toward the trail, maybe thirty feet away and there was a rifle in the boot. I walked up to him, talkin' soft, holdin' out a hand. The shiny brass of the rifle breech said it was a Henry '44, and I'da put my last dollar it was the rifle that killed Christian Pollock.

Walkin' back to the dead man I looked at the bottom of his boots. There was no slice in the left heel. Either he'd changed boots or someone else had left their mark up at the mine. I left the body there but undid the gun belt and pulled it loose. I walked back over to the horse, tied the gun belt to the saddle strings, then led the horse back toward the trail.

As I came down, I kept an eye out, but I could see no one else and I was bettin' there weren't more'n two of them. When we got to the trail I headed the horse down the mountain, slapped him hard on the rump, and he set off at a trot, down toward town. He'd find his corral, all right, I was sure of that. I was also pretty certain it would be at the Hoover ranch. Turnin' around, I walked up the trail toward the spruce thicket where I'd tied Tempter.

CHAPTER 15

For me it was a new world. I'd been almost too small to remember havin' a home I belonged to. Maybe the nearest thing, I guess, had been the winter with the Cheyenne – but livin' with Indians, that's different. Lawyer Miller, he fixed it so's I could move into Pollock's cabin right away.

There wasn't much in the cabin by the way of fixin's, furniture and the like. But the cabin was pretty as any I'd ever seen. It was made of peeled ponderosa logs that'd been notched mighty careful to the cabin could be tightly chinked. It would be snug for the winter, all right.

The big livin' room had a cook stove and a kitchen at one end, and off the livin' room was a second room that Pollock'd built as a bedroom, but mostly he just kept it filled with odds and ends of junk.

One of the first things I did, I cleared out that room, and I built me a double bed made out of logs, with stretched rawhide strips that Hans Mueller sold me. And I ordered up a good mattress for it, from out of Denver. I had in mind not bein' a bachelor much longer.

Ownin' that place was more enjoyable than most anything I could think of, and many a night I silently thanked poor old Chris Pollock for havin' give it to me. Right off, I wanted to be sure just what it was I owned, and I got a surveyor come down from Oroville to set up the boundaries proper. Especially, I wanted to know the line where my land and the Hoover spread came together.

I had scores to settle with Hoover, I'd no thought otherwise, but I didn't want any settlement brought about because of an argument about boundary lines. My fight with the Hoovers was more important than that, and some day it would explode. But for the moment at least, Hoover and his men stayed out of my way.

When I'd brought Pollock's horse and Balky, his mule, back down from the mine, I checked in with Ben Little, the sheriff, and told him about bein' shot at, and how I'd killed the man, and that there was another rider I heard comin' back to town. Little just shrugged his shoulders.

"You got any idea who put that man up to it?" he asked me.

"Not any more'n I know who killed Christian Pollock," I said. "Somebody wanted Pollock dead, and looks like someone wanted me dead, too. I don't even know whether it was the same person."

I never mentioned the rifle to him, just as I hadn't said anything after Pollock died. I was hopin' it might show up again.

"Well, I'll look into it, Krieger," he said.

"I'll ride back up there with you, sheriff, if you want help in findin' the body. Just stop at my place and we can ride there in two or three hours." But I never really expected him and I was right, he never came. I figured Ben Little could have found the name of the gunman who lay dead in the spruce grove, just by askin', and he knew the right person to ask.

After I moved into the cabin, I sometimes came across Brady Hoover or his son ridin' into or out of town. Tim did his best to ignore me when we'd pass. He was almost always with a cowhand or two. Once in a while I'd hear about how the

Hoover hands, Tim with them, would get wild drunk at the Mother Lode.

Brady Hoover, though, he was a strange one. He never seemed to carouse, and he stuck straight to business. I doubt I ever saw him smile, even. He had no small talk, and whatever warmth there might have been in his body, it looked like it evaporated years ago. I learned part of the story of Hoover over whiskey one night at Doc Train's. Mike O'Malley, Hans Mueller, Doc and I were all together there.

It was Mueller began the story, 'cause he'd know Hoover longer'n any of the rest of us. "I guess I saw him ven he first came to town," Mueller explained to us in his precise English with its thick German accent. "It vas right at the start, maybe ten years back. It vas certainly before the war began. I vas the last of the mountain men, still makin' my liffin' by trapping beavers up the Topaz Creek. Momma and me, ve had built a kind of sod hut into the edge of the chalk up on the north side of town. Only there vasn't yet any town there. You can still see the hut, it's there but it's already falling apart.

"The hut faced south and ve had it covered vith rocks and dirt so ve didn't freeze in the vinter. It vasn't much of a home, but Momma had our first two babies there. Beaver trappin' held good for a few years then und I made a few dollars. Because I felt Alta Vista vould grow, as soon as I could, I built our log house, and then the shop. A good thing, too, 'cause Momma kept havin' babies, and not any more would fit into the dugout.

"Ve vas chust settled into the house ven Hoofer rode into town. I remember he vas ridin' a Morgan like he rides now, and that vas the first Morgan I'd ever seen, and aftervards I realized it fit Hoofer vell. It vas a dainty horse, looked like it could never make it in the mountains. But after you got to know that horse, you knew it vas tough. Hoofer, he vas the same vay.

"He asked could he rent the dugout for the summer, und he did. The Senate Hotel vasn't built for maybe, vat, four years later.

"Hoofer rode around the valley a few days, on his Morgan, und asked questions about land. Anyone he talked to knew right soon he'd never been a rancher. Later on, a man came into the shop vunce, needed some harness fixed up. He'd drifted into town from Denver, said he knew Hoofer there, that Hoofer'd been a gambler, und he'd left town after he killed a miner, supposed to have been over crooked cards.

"Hoofer was in the hut maybe two weeks ven he came into the shop, said he vas riding back to Denver for his family. Irene, she came back up vith him and Tim, too. Tim he vas about eight then – he's the age of my Erich. They came in with a loaded buckboard. Irene, she vas driving the buckboard. Hoofer, he vas on the Morgan, and Tim, he had a pony of his own. A vagon brought up a load of stuff later after the house got built. They never seemed short of money in those days, and he hired Max Trelawney to build their house. Paid him vell und fair.

"It's funny, he could've had the ground Chris Pollock bought later. That Stan Samson, he'd filed on it, and lived out there in a cabin Chris tore down. Hoofer, though, he didn't know enough about land to know how valuable that vater there vas.

"It vas clear very quickly that Irene knew most of nothing about living out here.

She told Momma vunce she'd been a dance hall girl, come to Denver from St. Louis. She loved pretty clothes, jewelry, und good times."

"What became of her?" I asked.

"Doc Train, he knows that part better'n I do," Hans said.

"I'd just opened my office, Krieger, close to four years ago. Irene showed up one afternoon, walking stiffly and complaining about a sore back. I thought she meant she'd sprained something, but when I examined her, I could understand why her back was sore. She'd been badly beaten, and her back was a mass of welts. There wasn't much I could do for the poor woman, but I did tell her that if she allowed her husband to continue beating her, he might eventually kill her. She had more gumption than I gave her credit for, or maybe just more fear. I don't know.

"In any case, she walked out of my office, the stage for Denver was loading in front of the Senate. She bought a ticket, got onto the stage, and so far as I know, nobody in Alta Vista, including her husband, has seen her since. No matter where she is, I'd guess she's likely better off than she was with him.

"He and Tim, they live out there on that ranch and make do for themselves. They've got a Chinese cook, and he feeds them and keeps the place livable. But so far as I know, Hoover's never had another woman out there. That boy, as you've found out, Krieger, has grown up thinking he can do whatever he wants, and his old man will back him up."

Mike O'Malley spoke up. "Funny thing," he said. "When he came here, Hoover seemed to have lots of money, but he bought some of the poorest cattle I've ever seen. I've watched cattle of his bein' driven to Denver to sale, and they were mostly skinny critters he'd a been better off to've shot along the way.

"Then, maybe more'n a year back, maybe two years, he began to get cattle that looked mostly Hereford. I'd have to say I've never seen much better stock than those. He doesn't do very well by them, but if you start with good animals it's hard to ruin them in a couple of years.

"No one knows whether he makes money, except he pays his bills. He keeps to himself. Only ones he ever talks to are his son and his cowhands. With the rest of us here in town, he's mighty close mouthed. I agree with Mueller, he's like that Morgan. He's got a gambler's thin wrists and all, but underneath he's steel. Don't ever trust him, Krieger. Sometime Hoover'n you are goin' to have it out, and just don't ever offer him a chance."

What Mike said was right, of course. Hoover's anger had been whetted up sharp like a Green River knife, but like that knife, it just got kept in a sheath. It was sharp, and it was still there, and it was ready to kill. But it was hidden.

Hoover came ridin' in toward town one day just as I was ridin' back home. I never wore a gun in town now, and when Hoover and I passed, and he spoke to me, my gun hand kind of itched. I stopped Tempter and turned around to face Hoover. He talked soft like, and he began calm enough.

"I've been meaning to speak with you, Krieger. You know I wanted that property of yours when Pollock was alive. That stubborn old man would never sell to me. I just want you to know I still want to buy it. I need the water, and I'll pay you a fair price."

He was silent for a minute then, and when he spoke up again, his voice was different. "Krieger," he continued, "you're nothing but a wanderer, and you'll never settle down. Sell the land while you have a chance."

That last part got to me. I didn't like any man tellin' me what I was or wasn't, least of all Hoover. "The property's not for sale, Hoover!"

I could feel his anger gettin' the best of him. "I'll have it some day!" he almost shouted at me. He just couldn't bear to be crossed, that man.

"Maybe you will, maybe you won't, Hoover. You might have to decide if it's worth killin' for!"

He looked me up and down, never said a word more, then turned his horse and trotted on in toward town. I don't think we ever talked again, not until several months later, and when we did then, it was more Hoover talkin' than me. And he had decided by then that I was right. I would have to be killed.

Tim Hoover, he just ignored me. But I knew that our days of ignorin' each other would have to end sometime. 'Specially after I found out about the boots. Hans Mueller stopped me as I was tyin' Tempter in front of the Weintraub's store one day.

"Krieger," he said to me. "We talked once about a pair of boots..."

I nodded, understandin' all right what he meant.

He continued, "The pair you wanted to know about, vell, it's in my shop right now. You walk up with me, I'll show you. I'm glad I found you," he said as we walked toward the shop. "I promised to put on new heels. He said he would come back tomorrow. You can see the boot."

The one time I'd been to Denver I'd seen boots like these. They were the softest plain fine leather I could imagine. Cowhands spend money on women, gamblin', liquor, saddles, and boots, but I knew no cowhands could afford leather like that, even if they gave up all the other things. They were well worn, but they still had a richness I couldn't put into words. These boots were somethin' special.

I picked up the left boot, turned it over, and there was no doubt about it. It seemed impossible that the mark at the mine, which had been burnin' in my memory all this time, could have been made by any other boot. I looked at it a minute, my mind fillin' up with hate. Then I looked over to Mueller.

"The young Hoover!" he said simply.

It was no surprise, but at least I knew for sure that it had been Tim Hoover was up there with the killer, and it was him carried Chris Pollock's body up to the mine.

There was no pleasure I'd ever had like settlin' into that farm. I made maps, read books about crops. Once I even rode into Denver to learn what I could about water, who owned it, and how to use it. Everybody was helpin' me. Doc Train loaned me books. Hans Mueller, who seemed to know about everything, he helped me design how my irrigation ought to work.

And Erla O'Malley, she taught me to bake pies. Once, after I'd baked an apple pie at home, followin' the directions she wrote out for me, I saddled Tempter and rode into town with the pie, still in its pan and covered with a cloth, carryin' it balanced in the flat of my hand. I rode up the length of Main Street to the O'Malleys and presented it to Erla. Colleen was standin' there, laughin' at me, and mostly I guess I wanted to grab her and kiss her while she was laughin'. I just never felt anything like this about life, and it was at that time, in spite of the Hoovers, when I felt the world was mine.

Colleen and I were married just after Christmas. I had asked permission of Mike O'Malley, and he just clapped me on the shoulder and said, "Krieger, I thought ye'd never ask. But to be politic, ye'd best ask Erla, too."

She was delighted, but she was worried about where we could find a priest in the middle of winter in a tiny village in the Rocky Mountains.

Then, finally, I asked Colleen herself. I'd not been certain she'd really understand about marriage, with all she'd been through. But Erla'd talked with her, and as I so often did, I loved that woman, but I never reckoned just how smart she really was. She understood clear enough, and her answer was yes.

When I asked her to marry me, we'd been out ridin' together and had gotten off our horses and were sittin' on a big round rock in the winter sunshine, out east of town where there was little snow. When I asked her, she just looked up at me, very serious like, then reached out and put her arms around my neck, and we kissed and she pulled me closer to her, and well, I knew that's what I'd been waitin' for.

There wasn't much I knew about weddings. Since there was no church had yet been built in Alta Vista, Erla decided we should be married in their front room. She was still frettin' about the priest, and it was Doc Train solved the problem, kind of.

"It's just as simple as this, Erla," he explained to her. "You'll have to without a priest, or without a wedding. I don't think you'll keep those two apart for long, so you'd best settle for no priest. The nearest Catholic Church is more'n a hundred miles away. Why don't we get them married now, as best we can, and then next summer they can go down the valley and be married again – by a priest in the Hernandez village, San Badillo."

He had more to offer. "Here in Alta Vista we may not have a priest, or even a recognized minister. But if Hans Mueller was capable of buryin' Chris Pollock in the fashion he did, he certainly ought to be able to marry Krieger and Colleen."

"Hans Mueller?" Erla was pretty shocked by the idea, I guess. But Mike talked with her, and she didn't have many choices anyhow, and it was Hans Mueller married us.

It was pretty crowded in the O'Malley front room, what with most the town there. I don't guess there's any other place in the world a weddin' like that could have been. I looked across and there was Colleen, a tall, dark, black haired Ute Indian. I was a blond Pennsylvania German. Our best man was a doctor, come from Harvard University. The man who married us had been a beaver trapper and was now a cobbler, a tinkerer, and a designer of irrigation for my farm. He was also a minister. At least, he managed that weddin' in a right dignified way.

I looked to the guests just before we were wedded, and most of the women were cryin' quietly. All of them had crossed the United States, and a good many of them, like Momma Mueller, had crossed the Atlantic Ocean, and most of that travelin' had been pretty tough for anyone, man or woman. But they could still cry at a weddin'. I noticed the men were clearin' their throats from time to time, too.

It'd been snowin' all day long, one of those silent snowstorms without any wind we have here in the middle of the Rockies. The snow piles up on trees, the mountains, and on all the rooftops in town. After the weddin' Colleen had changed from her weddin' dress into deerskin trousers, and when the festivities were gettin' close to finished, we went outside. She mounted the pinto and I climbed onto Tempter. The Mueller kids were standin' there in the snow storm, throwin' rice at us.

We rode out of town, just as the softness of twilight was settlin' in with the snowstorm, and went on up to the cabin. The snow continued for most of two more days, but we hardly knew about it for we never took time to look out. When a

Chinook swept down off the mountains and melted off the snow, we figured we had no more excuse to stay to ourselves, so we saddled up and rode back to town, workin' our way through the snowdrifts.

The next month, well, there was never anything like it. We rode the farm, I pointed out what fields were gonna be where, and how we would bring irrigation water down from the mountains. The snow cover up high was so heavy that sometimes we could hear the roar of avalanches up above, and I figured there'd be plenty of water for farmin' this year.

Colleen loved takin' the horses off to the east, across the Arkansas to where there was little snow. We rode over there one mornin', turned south from the wagon road to Denver, and went down through a narrow windin' valley with big round sandstone boulders. This was dry country, with scattered pinon and once in a while some ponderosa up on the higher hills. It wasn't land belonged to anyone, but the Hoover cattle used it for winter grazin', and there were small bunches of cows and yearlin' heifers eatin' on the dry winter grass.

We came up over a rise. Colleen was in the lead, and she reined in the pinto and motioned for me to come up alongside. Not more'n a hundred feet beyond us we could see the carcass of a cow, and tearin' at it was a cougar with three cubs. I reached for my Winchester, but Colleen put out her hand to stop me. I guess she figured even cougars had a right to live, though she knew how tough they were on cattle.

I slid the Winchester back into the boot, and Colleen nudged the pinto off the trail, through the rabbit brush over toward the cougar. We were downwind, and when the pinto caught the lion scent, he bucked a little, uneasy. But Colleen, she never had trouble sittin' a horse.

But the cougar saw us then, and she snarled at us, and the dark tip of her tail was the only thing on her that moved. The cubs, they got some sort of command from her somehow, and they froze, too. I thought for a minute she might do battle over the carcass, and I was ready to go for the Winchester. But she turned and loped through the brush toward the red rocks, the cubs taggin' along right behind. She most likely had a den up there somewhere.

We rode on up to the cow, and I got off to see how that cougar'd been workin' on it. I knew she wouldn't eat tainted meat, and she'd just made the kill there, the blood hadn't even had a chance to dry up yet. It was a bony, skinny cow all right, maybe sick from the winter. She carried the Double Circle Double H brand that belonged to the Hoovers.

Back in here, I figured varmints like that cougar must cost Hoover a lot of cattle. A bunch of ravens were already movin' in closer, squawkin' like they do. They'd been kept away by the cougar bein' there. We couldn't see coyotes, but they'd be near somewhere, waitin' their turn.

I was all ready to mount up when somethin' about that brand stuck in my mind. Walkin' back over to the cow, I studied the brand again. The Double Circle Double H brand looked like it'd just been burned on last fall, and it wasn't completely healed, maybe 'cause the cow was sick or somethin'. But underneath part of it there was an old scar.

It was the Circle R! That cow had been over branded. She'd once belonged to Pete Chalmers and the Circle R! I doubted it made sense. But lookin' again, there were no doubts. The old scar at the top of the left H was plain as could be. At one time that had been an R!

I thought on that a minute, then I took my knife and cut a square with the brand away from the rest of the hide and scraped the flesh off. Then after I thought about it I cut the remainin' hide around the bare spot into strips and roughed it up some, so it might look like cougar damage, just in case any of Hoover's cowboys happened across the carcass.

The fleshy side of the hide was all sticky with blood, and I picked up some sand and rubbed it to dry it off before I walked over to Colleen, who'd been watchin' the ravens. I told her about the double brandin', and the Circle R brand bein' underneath.

This single hide wasn't that much evidence, but we rode on and found five more cows standin' in the lee of a rock cliff. We rode in slow and quiet, so's not to spook them too much. The whole damn bunch was the same, no question. They'd been changed. As Mike O'Malley'd said that night we were talkin' about Hoover, he'd been getting' better cattle of late. He sure had, they were cattle run off from the Circle R.

If it was Trigger Watson was rustlin' the Circle R stock, then at least some of them must be comin' up here over some mountain trail on Poncha Pass. I figured after the brand was all healed, Hoover could sell this stock in Denver, no questions asked. It was a pretty slick operation, I'd have to hand it to him.

As we rode out of the valley I was thinkin' what my next step'd oughtta be. I couldn't go to the sheriff. Ben Little was no man to trust. And I finally decided I'd best just sit on this for a week or so. Those cattle weren't goin' to be moved off the range very quick, not until the cows had calved and the calves were old enough to trot the trail by themselves. Maybe there was somethin' more I could learn.

It wasn't until later I found out about Tim Hoover. He was already dead by then, and his daddy was tryin' to kill me. But from what I learned then, while we'd been workin' on that cow that'd been killed by the cougar, Tim Hoover must o' been up in the ponderosas, tryin' to locate strays. When he saw me and Colleen ride up to the dead cow, he likely watched until we disappeared back toward the Denver road, then came on down to the cow. He'd o' been smart enough to know the difference between where my knife'd cut the hide away, and where the cougar'd been workin'. And as it turned out, he knew right away why we'd taken the hide.

When we rode up the trail to our place, Hans Mueller's wagon and team were drawn up in front of the cabin. He was pretty upset.

"Krieger!" he began, and his excitement made his accent worse. "In town, I vas at the Mother Lode hafing a schnapps before I went back home this afternoon. There vas this cowboy there vis some others from the Hoofer ranch. He vas very drunk, and Krieger, he said he'd come here to kill you. He said...he said vunce he owned Colleen, who is now your vife...and that she vas his woman! Vhat kind of talk is that, Krieger?"

But Mueller didn't wait for an answer. He went on, and I had trouble followin' him. "He said you'd killed his brother, and now he meant to kill you."

Colleen was listenin', and she understood right away, and she put her hand on my arm and looked up at me.

"Trigger Watson!" I said, and I took a deep breath while I thought over what I had to do.

"Drunk or sober," I finally said, "He's too dangerous for me to ignore. I'll go to town. Hans, thank you for comin' out here. It would be better, I think, if you could stay until I get back. Colleen might be in danger here by herself."

Hans understood. Colleen set to takin' the saddle off the pinto, and I went into the house to buckle on my gun belt and check the Colt. I kissed Colleen, mounted Tempter, and rode toward town.

When I found Trigger Watson, he was sittin' on the edge of the wood walk in front of the Mother Lode. He'd had far more whiskey than he could manage. His friends must o' been inside, still drinkin', I figured. I'd heard enough about Watson that I knew it was him sittin' there. I tied Tempter across the street and walked over to Watson. He was a sorry sight.

He raised his head and looked up at me. "Ha!" he said, "You're Krieger!" He tried to get up, and he reached slowly and not very steady for his gun. A baby could've gone faster'n Watson. I hit him square in the face, and I felt the gristle of his nose smash. His head snapped back and he slumped down onto the ground. He didn't move. I walked up to him and rolled him over with my foot. I pulled his Colt out of the holster, opened it and scattered the cartridges on the street, then threw the gun as far as I could up the street.

Walkin' past him, I swung open the doors into the Mother Lode. There was one of Hoover's men in there, and a cowboy I didn't remember ever seein' before, and I moved across to them.

"When that drunken bum out front recovers, you take him back to the ranch. If I ever see him in town or near my place, I'll kill him. No questions, no draws, just dead. And you be sure to tell him, when he's sober enough to understand, that the next time it won't make any difference to me whether he's drunk or sober. You understand that?"

"Yessir!" said the Hoover cowboy. I figured he could tell how mad I was.

The second man said nothin', and I felt he'd oughtta carry the message too. He just continued to look at me. I grabbed him by the shirt.

"You understood me?" I shouted. I moved closer to him, 'til my face was only a couple of feet away from his, and his back was bein' pushed against the bar.

"I understand, Krieger," he said finally. "But I'm carryin' lead in my leg, and you put it there one day at the Circle R. And by God, I'll get you for it sometime!"

"Don't try it!" I warned. He didn't, not then. I let go of his shirt, turned and walked out the door, past Watson, who was still lyin' there. I got Tempter and rode back home.

Nothin' had been settled, I knew that. But it was in the open now. Watson was here in Alta Vista, he had some connection with Hoover, and that cowboy with the bum leg, he'd been there at the Circle R. I figured before it was over, either Watson or me would likely be dead. I intended it to be

Watson. But I didn't know then how fast it was goin' to move.

CHAPTER 16

It wasn't more'n a couple of days I saw Trigger Watson again, and that was at a distance. Afterward, I was never all sure exactly what had happened. It was hard to get it from Colleen, and before it was all done, everyone else involved was dead.

When I heard the shots I was half a mile below the cabin, measurin' up what was to be a grain field, poundin' stakes into the frozen ground. There was a bunch of firin', followed by shoutin', and what sounded like drunken "Yahoos!" The shots carried like revolvers, and they had to've come from up by the cabin.

Tempter was tied just about ten feet from me. I dropped the stakes and the sledge, ran to where he was, and we galloped across the field toward home. I'd gone only a few seconds when there were two more shots, clearer this time, and they sounded like the Winchester.

When I got up to the front door I could see, at the far end of our lane, and movin' fast toward town, there were two horsemen. One seemed to be supportin' the other.

I shouted "Colleen," got off Tempter and dropped the reins. I ran to the front door. It was part way open and Colleen was standin' inside, still holdin' the Winchester in both hands.

Seein' me, she lowered the gun, and moved out the door toward me. She put her arms around me, and put her head on my chest. She was tremblin'.

"Who was here? What happened?"

She looked up at me, and if only she could have talked...No one had ever bothered her since we moved to the cabin. It had to be somethin', someone..."Trigger Watson!" I shouted.

She shook her head yes. "But there were two of them," I said.

She knelt on the ground, picked up a twig, and quickly drew two circles. Before she got the first H put in, I knew.

"Tim Hoover!" I made it sound like a question, but I already knew the answer. I remembered their shoutin'. "They were drunk and wanted you! Which one was shot?"

She pointed to the brand. "How bad was he hit?" She shrugged, and took me a few feet farther out from the door. There was a big stain of blood on the ground there. It had spread into some old snow that was lyin' by a rock.

I could see nothin' but trouble ahead. It was almost dark now, and I figured we'd do better to wait in the cabin, rather than my stirrin' things up by goin' to town. I tied up tempter but left him saddled, then took Colleen into the almost dark cabin, and bolted the door. She struck a match to light a lamp, but I stopped her and blew out the match.

"We're better off in the dark," I said. I found a box of cartridges for the Winchester, and I walked over and picked up my gun belt and buckled it on. We sat quiet after that, watchin' our road, and the road into town. I put my hand over hers.

"I'm sorry I wasn't here," I said. "We'll work it out all right. And somehow or other we'll get rid of them both..."

But I had little idea what might happen next. One thing I was almost sure of. The time for talk was gone. Guns were goin' to make the speeches from now on. I figured if Tim Hoover was shot, and was maybe even dead, Brady Hoover would be a madman. That kid was a mess, but he was the only thing Brady Hoover had left in life.

Trigger Watson would try to make it worse. Not that he gave a damn about Colleen, not after the way he'd used her. But he was out to get me, 'specially after I smashed his face when he was drunk, but refused to kill him then. Maybe I'd made a mistake.

We needed to hear more of anyone comin', so I unbolted the door and left it part open. There wasn't much snow in the valley, but we felt the cold pretty quick. It wasn't a long wait, though. There were hoof beats of a single horse in a few minutes, comin' in our road, gallopin' hard. I drew my Colt, and stood by the door, watchin'. The rider wasn't tryin' to keep quiet, and it was dark enough now I couldn't see much at that distance. But when the hoof beats were still maybe a hundred feet down the lane, the horse slowed to a trot, and a voice shouted "Colleen! Krieger!"

It was Mike O'Malley.

"Come on in!" I shouted. I was anxious to let him know we'd recognized him. But I kept my gun out until I could see it was Mike's big sorrel. He dismounted and tied the horse beside Tempter.

"We've got problems," Mike began, as he stepped into the house. "They're gonna take mighty quick solutions. Listen to me! Tim Hoover's dead. He dropped off his horse just this edge of town. They carried him to Doc Train, but he was already gone. His old man was in town already, along with a couple of the Hoover cowhands, loadin' up supplies to go back to the ranch.

"Best I can tell, Watson says they were just passin' your place when Colleen let fire with the rifle and hit Hoover twice."

"That's a damned lie, Mike. The two of them were tryin' to break into the cabin to get at Colleen. They must've been mighty drunk. I was down in the lower meadow. She shot Tim Hoover not ten feet outside the door. His blood's still on the ground there."

"I knew it had to be like that, Krieger, but that's not the story Watson's tellin'. They've already got half the bums in town with them, and they'll be ridin' up to the

Hoover ranch to get others. Then they'll be back here in force pretty quick, and they're not gonna be askin' questions or lookin' for blood on the ground. Hoover's got them all riled up. When they come out here, there'll be shootin', not talkin'."

I realized how bad it was. "Where's Ben Little?"

"Him? He was in town 'til he heard the story, then he disappeared. Don't look to him. He'll not be back until Hoover gives the word. Doc Train, of course, knows about it, and he's ready to fight. So's Hans Mueller, though I don't know about him with a gun. And some of the other folks are on their way out here.

"But, hell, Krieger, Hoover will have at least twenty men of his own. You get a mob like that, there's no reasonin' at all. They'd love to string up a white man with and Indian wife. I'm goin' back to town to meet the others. We'll fight them on the road, try to keep them out of here.

"If they get here, Hoover'll see to it they either shoot you down or take you prisoner. And you know how far either of ye'll get as a prisoner!"

This was more serious now than just Colleen and me. I knew that. In a battle like Mike was talkin' about, half the people in town might end up dead. I couldn't let that happen, not nice as they'd been to me. I made up my mind quick.

"You'll do no fightin', Mike! None of you! Colleen and I are goin' to run!"

"Run away?" I guess the thought'd never occurred to Mike O'Malley.

"Mike, winterin' among the Cheyennes, I learned no one ever argued about their courage. But they figured the odds. When things got too tough, they turned and ran. That way they were alive for the next battle, when maybe the odds were better. You stand up to Hoover and half the good men in Alta Vista might end up killed. And likely so would we. I say it's damn foolishness. Colleen and I can load our horses and in ten minutes we can be gone."

But Mike, he was still havin' trouble with the idea. "Where'll ye go? There's nowhere they won't eventually catch up with ye."

"With any luck, Mike, it'll be daylight before they can find our trail. By then they might be sober enough they won't want to follow. We'll go back up around Alta Vista and take the trail up Sunshine Pass to the cabin up at the mine. We can pack enough food to make out a few days, and the place is built like a fortress if it comes to that. We can wait 'em out up there."

"Ye'll never get horses up that trail through the snow."

"We can damn well try, Mike. If it gets too deep for the horses we can take to snowshoes and chase the horses back down here. We can fight Hoover off forever up there. They'll quit and come back to town after a few days of the cold." I was losin' patience havin' to explain. Time was too important to be standin' there arguin'.

"But up higher, Krieger, that's just one big avalanche path, and with the snows hangin' on like that…"

I lit a lamp and began to pack things from around the house, and Colleen understood, she was readyin' food.

"We'll just have to take our chances, Mike. We're goin' to do it. We'll be up there before mornin'."

"It's a hard ride," he said, but I knew he was agreein' we should go. "You get saddled up and on your way. I'll ride out toward the Hoover place and when that gang comes back they'll at least stop to talk with me for a few minutes. That'll give you a mite more time. But it's not much."

I remembered then. "One thing before we go, Mike, and it's important. You'd better know this in case...well, Colleen and I found a dead cow over in Squaw Gulch, where Hoover's been runnin' cattle on winter pasture. That cow'd been over branded. The Double Circle Double H brand had been burned over a Circle R brand. We checked a handful of other cows up there, and they're the same.

"It was a good job, but the old brand's still plenty clear. Take this hide and if we don't get back, see word gets down to Pete Chalmers at the Circle R. Trigger Watson's been here in town, and he's been with Hoover's men. He's the one's been rustlin' the Circle R cattle for Hoover."

Mike, he held Colleen a minute, then he turned to me and shook my hand and said, "Good luck!" Then he turned and went out the door.

It would o' been a help if we could have brought Polly, but with a load she'd have foundered soon's she reached the deep snow. I tried to remember what had been left in the cave. I remembered the dynamite and a keg o' flour. If we had any luck, killin' a deer wouldn't be hard. If the weather held 'til mornin', once we were at the mine we could survive most anything.

But between our cabin and the mine, if it came onto a bad storm, it might just kill us. Down where we were startin' out, it was only a bit below freezin', but the climb would be almost to timberline, and up there I figured it was below zero already.

When we got both horses loaded, we put pack baskets on our own backs and mounted up. Ridin' side by side so our trail would be clearer, we headed southeast across open ground 'til we came to the stream. It was still full of ice, but there was some open water runnin' too.

We went into the water, headed down, then turned around and came back up for about a quarter mile. I figured they'd not find our tracks 'til mornin' comin' out of the stream, and the first direction we'd taken would indicate we'd made off toward the Denver road. But they weren't fools, and sometime they'd find where we'd come out, goin' up the mountain. It might pick us up a few minutes, or maybe several hours. If we didn't fool them at all, and they found our tracks right tonight, they'd have to go back to the ranch or into town and pick up gear for the mountains. I didn't reckon there was anyone fool enough to come up that trail without winter gear, followin' us at night, unless maybe it would be Brady Hoover.

We had a hard time with both Tempter and the pinto. They didn't much like walkin' in the dark through the rocks in that icy stream. Once we came out above, though, both the horses settled into a good trot. I never pushed them, for I figured it was goin' to be a long, hard ride, and we had a good lead.

The first few miles made it seem easy enough. There was part of a moon up above, the air wasn't cold enough to frost us, and we made good time. But I wasn't fooled. I knew the worst was up ahead. It was around midnight the moon disappeared into clouds and I could feel the snow comin' on. We must have been half way to the mine – the easy half, it turned out.

Most places now there was close to two feet of snow on the ground. We passed the beaver pond where I'd killed the man who carried the Henry. Whatever was left of him was buried up there in the snow up by the rock slide. Old Ben Little never did look into that one.

On beyond a ways we stopped and got off the horses. We were already stiff from ridin' and from worryin'. We built a small fire in a spruce grove, melted snow for tea and chewed on some stringy jerky we'd brought with us. But even though we heard nothin', I was uneasy, and we mounted up quick and moved on. Colleen was doin' well.

When the snow started up I figured we still had maybe three more hours of ridin'. The moon was long since gone, and it had cooled down enough that by now Colleen and me both had hid our faces behind neckerchiefs, with just our eyes out into the cold. The snow began quiet enough, but pretty soon I could hear a downslope wind rattlin' the tops o' the spruces. And with the wind I knew the snowflakes would begin to sting like needles.

I dug my heels into Tempter and he moved faster, but it was harder because the snow was deeper under foot now. Back when the moon was still out, I'd looked up the slopes for big overhangs, or for avalanches, but down below there'd been no bad slides. Up here it was snowin' too hard to see anything, and we'd simply have to run the danger, and pretty quick we found some of that.

Tempter stopped when he went belly deep in the snow, and I squinted out into the darkness ahead. There was a great mound of white, and for a minute I thought we'd lost our way off the trail. But finally I realized we were into an avalanche'd come off the mountains to the north some time back. I figured we might have to abandon the horses and try to continue the rest of the way on snowshoes. If we did that, I wasn't sure we'd make it, for the wind was gettin' worse all the time.

Reinin' Tempter off to the left, I found the snow got lower as we went, where the avalanche had played out across the valley. Colleen was tight behind me on the pinto. It was almost to the slope on the south before the tongues of the snow slide were flat enough that I could force Tempter up through.   It was tougher goin' for Colleen on the pinto. That horse just didn't have the legs for this deep snow.   Still, when the trail was broke by my big dun, the pinto managed.

Once we got above the avalanche, we worked our way back across the valley and picked up the trail again.   The snow everywhere now was so deep it was all the horses could do to keep movin'. I finally stopped and got off, but I signaled back for Colleen to stay on the pinto. I pulled the snowshoes from my saddle pack and tied them onto my boots. I had to take a minute to rub my fingers, 'cause they were about frozen, before I could get the snowshoes on.

Pullin' Tempter along behind me, I broke trail for him. It was snowin' so hard now I had to keep runnin' my gloves over my eyes, 'cause the snow was cloggin' up my seein'.   I turned around and looked back, and I could tell the pinto, even with the trail broken for him, was wearin' out. I figured we had less than a mile still to the corral, and I knew that if I had to, I could make it alone on snowshoes. I wasn't sure about Colleen, though.

The horses were belly deep most of the time now, and their breath was comin' in fierce quick snorts, like they do. It was both the effort of workin' through the snow, and we were up mighty high now. I stopped to give the horses a break and to catch a breath for myself. But I knew that if I stayed more 'n a minute or two, there'd be no goin' on. Where I'd stopped was among some lodgepole pine, and the snow wasn't so deep there.

When I looked back, Colleen was off the pinto and was puttin' on her snowshoes. I began to walk back toward her, but she put up her hand and motioned me to go on. She was right, without her weight the pinto would have it easier. But I hoped she could make it on foot. The cold was beginnin' to make me feel drowsy now. I remembered a winter in Montana when Pete Chalmers and I'd been caught in a quick storm and we'd been like this. We just wanted to go off to sleep.

Colleen was still movin' along, and I was forcin' myself to keep walkin'. I was goin' on with my head down, tryin' to keep my eyes freed from snow, when Tempter gave a short whinny and stopped. I pulled against the reins, but he balked. I looked up, and then I saw the edge of the corral fence. We were there!

Walkin' back to Colleen, I pointed to the fence. I guess she smiled, but all I could see was her eyes, and they were most covered with snow. I got Tempter the last distance up to the base of the cliff. When I looked down the valley behind us I could see the first glimpse of the mornin' light. We had ridden, walked, and fought the snow all night, and by God, we had made it!

Beatin' a snowshoe trail up the ledge to the cabin, I dropped my pack inside. It was still almost dark up there, but I could see it was dry inside. Colleen had come up the ledge, walkin' careful, for the snowshoes had made it seem even narrower. Inside, I pulled off my gloves and with my numb fingers I fished through my pockets and found a metal can of matches I was carryin'. We started a pitiful small fire in the stove, and in a few minutes the warmth made a big difference. Colleen took off her snowshoes and stayed in the cabin, but I turned around and went on down the ledge and in several trips I had the rest of the gear brought up.

Where the enclosure of the corral ended up against the cliff wall, a big area had been protected from the wind and snow, and I was sure the horses would be all right there for several days – they'd be able to paw down to enough grass to keep from starvin'. One way or another, I wasn't countin' on bein' here more than a few days. I unsaddled the horses, smacked them to start them over to the bare area, and then climbed back to the cabin.

It was light enough now that I could look up the valley, and I could see on the steep slope directly above us a great overhangin' edge of snow. Whenever it came down there would be an almighty big avalanche across the cabin and into the valley. As I went back up the ledge, I was thankful Chris and I had built the cabin front as solid as we knew how.

When I came into the cabin and closed the door behind me, Colleen was already meltin' snow in a pot on top of the stove, and I could sniff meat fryin'. The world began to look better.

As I figured it, the Hoover gang might be in the valley anywhere from late afternoon to sometime next day. Likely not too many would come, but they wouldn't travel light. That was just too dangerous up here. They'd get up here prepared to stay until both Colleen and me were dead. But I didn't think they'd be in any great hurry.

It would be kind of like a huntin' trip for them – only we were the animals they were huntin', and if they knew they had us cornered, they'd take their time, like treein' a cougar. We'd cornered ourselves, that was clear enough. I wasn't much worried, though. We had ourselves a pretty solid fort. The logs were close to a foot around, and no bullet could get through them. The door swung open onto the narrow ledge that sloped down to the valley floor, and a tiny window in the door gave us a view of anyone that might try to make it up the ledge. The window in front, that would get shot out the first action, but we'd have to put up with that when the time came.

Unrollin' our soogans, we climbed into bed. We were pretty bad done in, both of us. "Looks to me we can sleep safe to about noon," I said to Colleen. "After that, we've a lot of work to get done before sundown."

Sleepin' wasn't much of a problem, but like always, I had one ear open for trouble. I had to have some reason for each noise I heard. As we slept, the sky cleared off and the sun reached down into our side of the valley. We could feel it warmin' the cabin. When I woke up it was because there was some noise didn't make sense to me. Colleen was already sittin' up, lookin' around puzzled like.

The sound was almost, but not quite, like a storm comin' through the pines. But then, mighty quick, it became a great roll of thunder. It seemed like the cabin shook. The harsh sunlight that'd been comin' through the front window got all soft and kind of yellow. We'd both been out of our blankets at the first big roar, and standin' behind the front window, we watched up across the valley, up just beyond the mine entrance. The side of the mountain up there seemed to break away, and to slip down into the valley.

"Avalanche!" I shouted at Colleen. She shook her head. Trees, rocks, and snow blocked the upper valley twenty feet deep, and there was a cloud of powdery fine snow glinted way up I the sky – that's what had softened the light from the sun. It gradually cleared off.

We were awake now, so we set about plannin' for when Hoover would get up there. Usin' one of Colleen's snowshoes as a shovel, I cleaned off the walkway from the cabin, and Colleen put her snowshoes on then and set about gatherin' firewood. I thought we might need as much as several day's worth of wood stored away. Carryin' an axe, she went out toward the corral, found a couple of dead lodgepole pine that weren't buried too bad, and chopped them into stove length, then tossed them into her pack basket.

The horses were munchin' on dry grass when I went down to the corral. I unslung my Winchester and hiked back over to the main trail, then walked down maybe a quarter mile. On the north there was a narrow valley much like the one where our mine was. I looked along the cliffs and didn't much like all the snow that was hangin' there, but I felt I'd have to take the chance. I hadn't gone up the valley a hundred yards when I saw what I was after.

A deer, looked like a yearlin', was standin' in the lee of a ledge on the west side. The snow was shallower there. He was aware of me, all right, but he didn't seem either curious or afraid. But I knew better'n to take chances by tryin' to get in too close. I sighted the Winchester careful and squeezed off a shot. The explosion bounced off the canyon walls, and the deer dropped within a few feet of where it'd been standin'. Two other deer which had been restin' in the snow got up and moved away up the valley.

When I got up to him I saw my shot'd been a good one, and the yearlin' was already dead. I gutted the animal out and carved the haunches free and put them into my pack basket, then went back up toward the cabin. We wouldn't starve, not soon. By the time I got back, Colleen had already stored a large pile of wood in the back of the cave. I cut up the venison and said,

"We'd better fry up some of this while we have time. I'd a sight rather eat cold cooked meat than cold raw meat, and maybe we'll be too busy later on to do much cookin'."

Pickin' up stove wood, I noticed the dynamite box in the back of the cave, and I reckoned I didn't want any trouble from that. There was a kind of niche in the side wall toward the back, and I shoved it in there and covered it with the heaviest logs Colleen'd brought up. If there was shootin' – and that was most for sure – I didn't want any stray bullets mashin' into that dynamite. But I didn't want to just leave it outside somewhere either. I figured it'd be safe enough back there.

Lookin' out the window across the valley I guessed the first thing they'd do was pop the glass out with a few shots. We'd just not stand anywhere near that window while Hoover and his men were down there opposite us. So I found a place almost at the other end of the cabin where two logs hadn't met quite right when Chris and I'd built the cabin. I cut away the chinkin' and made two peep holes. I was figurin' they'd never notice those holes, and

Colleen and I'd always be able to look out, protected by the logs.

If they came up the valley, I saw no way we couldn't just wait them out. Hoover'd never be willin' to stay the winter, and I knew his cowhands would start to grouse about the cold, much as they wanted to get at Colleen and me. I was ready for them to come, and I wanted to get on with it.

Puttin' my snowshoes back on, I walked down below the cabin, out into the middle of the valley, just about where the man with the Henry had stood when he shot Chris Pollock. Those big round boulders out there were goin' to be good cover for Hoover's men. When they came up to them they'd be in the open for a few feet, but once they were behind the rocks there'd be nothin' we could do to them.

CHAPTER 17

It was right when I was about to go down to the corral to check the horses again that I heard Hoover's men. They were maybe a half mile down the valley, but they were comin'. I waited until the sounds were clearer, then I walked back up the ledge to the cabin. Colleen was still at the stove, cookin' up the venison. I told her they were in the valley, and she just nodded like it didn't matter. Looked to me as if there was maybe two hours before dark. They'd got up faster'n I'd figured. I wondered how many there'd be, but I guessed I'd know that soon enough.

We left the door part way open, and I could hear their horses down in the corral. They'd come ready for the cold, and it took them maybe fifteen minutes to unload their packs and set up some sort of camp down there.

The first move was theirs. Whatever was goin' to happen was about to start. I checked the Winchester, put out extra ammunition, and I buckled on the Colt.

Colleen had a second Colt, and I knew that if the time came, she was as good as me with either the Colt or the Winchester. The way I'd figured it out, they were goin' to move up to the boulders, almost opposite the cabin, bein' mighty careful not to be in the open much 'til they saw what kind of action we were goin' to take.

I'd already knocked out one of the lower panes in the window so's we could hear them better. It was temptin' to try to pick off one of them as they moved into position down below. But I thought it'd be better to let them take the first shot, and for them to feel secure that I wasn't shootin' at them right off. I watched through the peephole. I wasn't sure how many men had actually moved in among the rocks. Colleen had been at the other peephole, and I asked her how many. She held up her full hand. Five. They'd likely have left at least one man down by the corral. The time was getting' short now, and I wanted to get on with it, whatever happened.

It was Brady Hoover's voice broke the silence after they were settled in down among the rocks.

"Krieger!" We could hear him plain enough through the broken window, but I didn't answer. It came again, even louder.

"Krieger!"

"I hear you, Hoover!" As soon as I said it, there was a whole volley of shots, and the window panes went into a million pieces. Glass flew to the back of the cave. We'd figured on that. Most of the bullets smashed into the ceilin', but one of them, aimed lower' the rest, ricocheted off the rock clear in the back of the cave. That could be dangerous, but I didn't see there was much we could do about it now.

"Krieger!" shouted Hoover. "I just couldn't hear you very well through all that glass, and we've got a lot to talk about."

I heard his men laughin', and I was tempted to stop them with a bullet, but it would have done no real harm, and I saw no reason to spend ammunition. Talk would be cheap down there.

"We're goin' to keep firin' off and on, Krieger, so expect it. Now, listen to me."

"I'm listenin', Hoover." There wasn't much choice, but his voice riled me. What he was sayin' riled me even more.

"That Indian bitch in there with you is what we want. Send her out, we'll take her and go back down the mountain, and you're free!" I could feel my jaw tightenin' up, and I put my arm around Colleen so she'd be sure to know what I felt.

"What of her, Hoover?"

"We turn her over to the sheriff. After all, she did kill my son."

Trigger Watson had to be somewhere among those rocks, though I'd not been able to make him out as they ran up from the corral. I thought I'd better find where he was, and stop this bull from Hoover.

"Watson!" I shouted. "That deal all right with you?"

Seemed like a long silence, and I figured they were talkin' among themselves. Then a deep voice, not Hoover, spoke up.

"Hell, no, Krieger! That's no deal with me. You killed my brother. You know we ain't gonna let the girl go anyhow, so let's talk some sense. We're gonna kill both of you before we're through here."

It was Hoover spoke up again. "Watson's right, Krieger. You know damned well what to expect. And Krieger, you ought to know this, too. That day you were up in Squaw Gulch, Tim was watchin' you from up in the ponderosas. He told me about your discoverin' the Circle R cattle. There's no way we're going to let you tell Pete Chalmers about that, so you get killed too, along with the Indian. You're cornered up in that cabin, and we've got lots of time. We came with plenty of food and lots of whiskey, and we're ready to stay for a while. When we go back, we'll be goin' back alone."

"Hey, Krieger!" This was a new voice. "This is Matt Tolley. You remember I was in the bar the other day after you worked on Trigger Watson. I told you I'd get even for your smashin' my leg that mornin' down to the Circle R. Well, that's what I'm here for. I ain't forgot!"

That's the last we talked with them that night. It was cold in the cabin, all right, with that window out. But we could drop wood into the stove, and for some reason they never did take out the stove pipe with rifle fire. We moved our soogans up toward the cabin door, away from the danger of bullets. I was countin' on the cold wearin' them down, and it'd sure be a lot colder camped out down by the corral than up in our cabin with the fire goin'. I figured they'd be driven to some crazy attack, or they'd retreat back to town.

Where we were sleepin, the stove kept us warm enough. The only dangerous place I could see was up to the entrance door, and I didn't think even Hoover was crazy enough to try that – not yet, anyway. It was seventy five feet right out in the open, and then a heavy timber door to get through. Pollock and I'd never bothered with a latch on the inside of the door, but I was guessin' that'd be the last thing they'd try.

Still, I kind o' half slept and half kept awake. Colleen, I knew she was the same way. We heard noise and laughin' down in the camp most the night. Hoover likely kept to himself, but the rest of the men down there seemed to think they were on a huntin' trip.

When the sky above the cliffs to the east brightened up, I felt some better. Lookin' out the peephole, I couldn't see anyone out among the rocks, so I moved over beside the window and shouted, "You fellows out there have a good night?"

It took them a few seconds, then there was a lot of shootin', and the bullets came screamin' in through the window. It settled down quick, though. Colleen and I had some breakfast, and I ate mine lookin' out the peephole.

Must have been close to an hour later, when it was a lot brighter, I could see figures runnin' up behind the brush to the shelter of the rocks. They were still temptin' me, 'cause I knew I could pick off one or two as they went. But I was willin' to wait out what they were goin' to do, and I was sure they'd get more careless all the time if they didn't get fired on.

Hoover was back up there, and his voice, when it came across to us, was beginnin' to get me pretty mad.

"You pay attention to me, Krieger! We're gonna do some shootin' here, and when that's finished, if you're still alive, we'll talk some more, and tell you what we'll do next. You won't like it."

I could hear the men around him laughin' again. I hunched back in the corner, and Colleen leaned in against the logs at the far end, away from the window. It didn't seem much sense to me, for they already knew that shootin' like they'd done last night was just a waste of powder. And no matter how much ammunition they'd carried up, sometime they'd have to begin to hoard it.

The firin' began, and it seemed it'd never stop. They put lots of shots through the window, but they peppered the logs with lead too. Colleen and I was sittin' up against the logs, that seemed the safest place, but we could feel the bullets as they hit outside on the logs. I kept watchin' through the peephole, tryin' to figure it out, and Colleen was up at the other end against the front wall, out of the way.

There looked like three, maybe four, rifles firin' away, and I was watchin' the rocks carefully to see which ones had men behind them. While they were firin', they had to show themselves for just a second, and maybe sometime we'd have to take a chance o' tryin' to shoot back through the window. I wasn't countin' on that, though.

The answer to all that wasted ammunition came pretty sudden, and it made me feel like a damned fool. It almost killed us both, too. The cabin door swung open, yanked hard from the outside. There was a figure standin' in the doorway, and the roar of his gun made a hell of a noise inside the cabin. He couldn't have seen much, just fired into what must have been almost darkness for him. He fired once, then a second time. But before he got to the trigger a third time, I'd cut him down. He never even saw me in the shadows near the door, and my Colt caught him practically point blank.

It was Trigger Watson, and he crumpled down onto the ledge, with the door still open. I was cursin' bein' so dumb, but I'd have to give it to Watson. He had more nerve than I'd given him credit for. Once he'd started up along that ledge, he was sure of gettin' killed if we'd discovered him. But I was mad as hell at myself for bein' so stupid as to get caught in a trick like that.

I looked over toward Colleen, where she'd been sittin' in the far corner. She wasn't there! She was lyin' on the floor. She'd been hit! I crawled across the floor and reached across to her. She was still livin' all right, but there was a lot of blood up by her right shoulder. I checked quick to make sure no one else was comin' up that ledge behind Watson, then I pulled my knife and slit open her shirt and looked at the wound.

Colleen gritted her teeth as I moved my fingers around the hole in her shoulder. "See if you can move your arm," I said.

She moved it all right, but it must have hurt like hell, 'cause she winced every time she moved. The bullet likely smashed her shoulder some, but it didn't look to me like she would bleed to death. I was already pressin' my neckerchief against the wound.

"The bleedin' should..." I started to say. But I got no farther than that, not right then. Three bullets slammed into the ceilin' above where we were crouched. They had to've come in the open door, and I guessed by where they hit that they'd been fired from the bottom of the ramp. I had to stop it.

We'd both dropped flat. I crawled across the floor and lifted the Winchester from where it'd been sittin' against the front wall. Out in the rocks, they'd begun firin' through the door again and I looked around at Colleen. She'd dragged herself up against the wall again.

I was makin' my way to the open door, and I was countin' on Watson's body givin' me some protection. Another bullet zinged in through the door just as I raised up over Watson to look out. That bullet just cleared my head, but I saw the flash of the gun and I aimed the Winchester, usin' Watson as a rest. I squeezed off a shot, and a figure ran back through the trees toward the corral as I jacked another shell in, and I fired again as he ran. But I couldn't tell whether I'd done any good or not. I was still cursin' my havin' been stupid enough to let Watson get up to the door.

Backin' into the cabin some, I looked around. Colleen was sittin' up in the far corner. The neckerchief she was holdin' against her shoulder was shiny with blood, and I didn't much like that. The firin' from out front had stopped for now, but I knew those damned fools would keep puttin' shells through the open door.

With that door stuck open I felt pretty naked all right. I didn't want anyone else shootin' up from the bottom of the ledge. Somehow, I had to get Watson's body out of the doorway. His head and shoulders were lyin' inside the door, toward me. He was a big man, but I grabbed his shoulders and turned him over. Pushin' the door wider open, I shook him as best I could, 'til his knees dropped out over the edge of the walk, then with all the muscle I had, I shoved him across the ledge and he dropped to the valley floor twenty feet down. They were firin' from the front now, at the open door, but I was protected good enough. And havin' got rid of Watson, I reached up and pulled the door shut.

Scramblin' across the floor to Colleen, I kissed her. The bleedin' from the shoulder seemed some less now, but things had changed with her getting' hit.

I'd planned just to wait out Hoover and the rest. But with Colleen shot like that, I had to get the fight over with. Damn Watson anyhow! Doc Train ought to be takin' care of Colleen's shoulder right now, but we were a long ride from town, and we had to get ourselves out o' this mess first. And if that bleedin' didn't slow down more, she might never make it down the valley.

There had to be some way to end it today, soon. If I'd had enough time I was certain I could've picked off the men one by one 'til the rest gave up and went back down to town. But that'd take more time'n I had.

Colleen was shiverin' pretty bad now, and I helped her move closer to the stove. On account of the sunshine, I didn't figure her shiverin' was as much from the cold as from getting' shot. I crawled back into the cave to get some wood for the stove, and as I lifted a chuck of firewood, I saw the case of dynamite and knew that was my answer!

It was chancy all right, and it might not work, but if it did...we were free! Pullin' the box to the front of the cave, I ripped it open with my knife. That dynamite was still frozen, sittin' on the floor of the cave back away from the stove. It wasn't goin' to be worth a damn 'til it was warmed up. I had to take a chance on that. Pickin' up the fryin' pan, I put four sticks of dynamite in, just like they were sausages, then put the lid on and moved over to the stove.

"We'll get out of here," I told Colleen. "There's maybe some danger we'll get blown to pieces, but we'll chance it. She nodded at me, but I figured she'd not much idea what I was up to. With the fryin' pan on top of the stove, I watched it for a minute, then took it off and turned the sticks. The bottom side was warm enough. If I figured wrong, it was all over. I left the fryin' pan back on the stove another minute or so, then put it down on the floor. I was countin' on the heat from the pan warmin' up the dynamite gradual.

Goin' over to the peephole, I looked out. I had to know how many men were out there, but 'course they were hidden by the rocks. I crawled over to Colleen, still sittin' in the corner.

"This is goin' to be tough, I know it, but take your good hand, put the Colt up on the edge of the window and fire out in the direction of the rocks. Don't bother tryin' to aim at them. Keep your head below the window. Just so they know we're firin'." She nodded and got herself to her knees.

Lookin' out the peephole, I motioned for her to begin firin'. They took the bait all right, and I counted at least three guns that were returnin' the fire. We'd figured there were five men last night out there, and likely one back at the corral. I'd killed Watson, and if I'd been lucky enough to hit the man who shot into the open door, then everyone left was out there on the rocks. That was a comfortin' enough thought. Trouble was I didn't know was it right.

But judgin' by the shots, the men out there were where I needed them. If it worked, this would be the end, and I could get on with movin' Colleen down to Doc Train. If not...

The dynamite felt warm enough, I was pretty sure of that. I checked the blastin' caps and tied on a length of fuse and wrapped the whole thing tight as I could. I found a match over by the stove and took a look out the small window in the door. There was no one I could see, but they could o' been hidden back in the trees easy enough. I'd have to chance it.

Crackin' the door open a couple of inches, I waited to see whether it drew fire. There was no shootin'. I crawled over under the window to Colleen to tell her what she had to do. I took my Colt, loaded it up, and handed it to her. And I picked up her Colt, which she'd been firin', loaded it up and put it down beside her.

"I know you hurt like hell," I said, "but you've got to help again for just two minutes. When I tell you, start firin' just like before. Keep down, don't chance getting' hit! I'm hopin' they're goin' to pay a lot of attention to those bullets comin' their way. I'm goin' to open the door and heave the dynamite!" I saw her eyes widen, but she nodded a silent yes to me, and I wasn't real sure whether she understood what I was tryin' to do, but I didn't want to take time to explain more.

"Don't fire 'til I tell you to start. I have to get the fuse goin' first..." I moved back under the window, took hold of the dynamite, and struck the match on the stone floor. I nodded over to Colleen, then waited until they'd started firin' back before I put the match to the fuse. It sputtered, and I watched it a second, then ran over to the door, threw my shoulder against it, and raced outside and down the ledge maybe six feet.

Spinnin' around, I faced the snowfield up above the cabin, and heaved the dynamite with everything I had. It went up there in a long arc, and I watched the fuse smokin' as it went. It was beautiful. It disappeared into the snow, and I could only hope. A bullet thudded into the rock just beyond me, and I dove for the open door. There was hammerin' of bullets on the wall just behind me, and then I was safe inside, and the door was pulled shut behind me.

Runnin' across the floor now, I grabbed Colleen and took her with me clean to the back end of the cave. I was prayin' that dynamite was goin' to go off, and I thought my heart was beatin' almost as loud as the explosion would be.

Seemed like it would never go off, but when it came, the concussion from up the mountainside above our heads was so great that dust and small pieces of rock dropped off the ceilin' onto us. We were huddled together there, and I had a sinkin' feeling that maybe the dynamite goin' off was all that was goin' to happen, and that would help a bit.

Then suddenly it started up. The earth above us shook. It was a wild rumble, and from in the cave it wasn't like anythin' I'd ever heard before. It got bigger, and it seemed to last forever. The avalanche slid down right over the cabin, and as the snow at the start came down past the smashed window, there was a great fog come into the cabin, with snow crystals everywhere. It made me afraid we might get suffocated, and I dove across the floor and grabbed a blanket from the bedroll and put it over both of us. At least we could breathe that way.

The roarin' was still gettin' worse, and now it was more than snow. We could hear rocks slidin' down over the cabin roof. I doubted the logs would hold. It was a sound wilder'n anything I've ever heard. I held onto Colleen tight, tryin' not to make her shoulder worse, but figurin' if the cabin let go and we got buried, we'd at least be together. It must've continued for half a minute, maybe more, then it slackened off and stopped.

When I took the blanket away from overtop us, there was snow still swirlin' around the cabin, and the walls, ceilin', and floor was white with snow. But the roof had held!

Sometime durin' the slide the door had got pushed part way open against the bank of snow from the avalanche that was pilin' up on the ledge. The stove was sputterin' and smokin' 'cause the stovepipe got swept away right off, and the slide dumped snow right down into the stove.

Crawlin' across the floor, I looked out the peephole, but it was clogged from the snow. I went over and very careful looked out the bottom of the window. The sparklin' mist was still everywhere out there, but I could see there was snow clear across the valley. The snow was level almost up to the bottom of the cabin. The rocks with Hoover and his men had disappeared. There was twenty feet of snow and rubble on top of them. I picked up the Winchester and knocked the snow off it. Goin' back over to the window, I watched careful, squintin' in the brightness, lookin' for anything that moved. I'd already decided I'd kill anything I saw. But it was absolute quiet, and I decided no one had gotten away from the avalanche.

Colleen came over to the window, and I asked if she'd keep watchin' the snowfield out there. When I said to shoot anythin' that moved, she looked around at me and nodded her head yes in a way I knew I could count on. I handed her the Winchester, even though I wasn't sure how she'd manage with her shoulder the way it was.

I began to dig us out. It took me ten minutes of hard work before I had the ledge cleaned away enough so the door could swing open far enough that I could get up on top of the snow piled there. Tyin' on my snowshoes, I buckled on my gun belt and loaded the Colt again.

The thing was, if any of Hoover's men hadn't been hit by the avalanche, I figured they'd be waitin' for me to come out the door. But there was no way except to take the chance. Hurryin' on snowshoes is like tryin' to run in deep water, but I got off that ledge quick as I could, and I breathed a sight easier when I got down to the lodgepoles. The corral area hadn't got hit at all by the avalanche, and I took a quick look at the camp and the remains of the campfire that'd belonged to Hoover's gang. I couldn't see any life there.

Over in the corral, the avalanche had scared the horses away from the cliff where there wasn't much snow, and out into the meadow where the snow was deeper. I located Tempter and Colleen's pinto, and I counted six other horses. They might 've brought a packhorse – but they might not've.

Trigger Watson was dead, we'd heard three guns at the rocks, and that should've left only the man who fired from below the ramp. Unless, damn it, there was no packhorse. Then there'd be another man somewhere. He might be buried out there in the snow. Or he might not be.

I edged my way out toward the campfire. Just short of it I saw a body lyin' there. I drew the Colt and walked across the open space, lookin' both at the body and keepin' my eye on the white beyond it. With the tip of my snowshoe I moved the figure and rolled him over. It looked like he died from a shot to the stomach – that'd have been my first shot, when he was still facin' up the ledge toward me. But he'd made it back as far as the campfire, for all the good it did him. He was the cowboy I'd made to swallow the lye soap at the Mother Lode.

While I was still lookin' at him, a shot echoed up through the canyon, and I dove for protection. That isn't easy with snowshoes on, but I made it behind a big spruce log pretty quick. Another shot hit the log. I figured the fire had come from the far side of the canyon openin', likely below where the avalanche ended. It was maybe a hundred and fifty feet from me. It would be a long shot for my Colt.

What I couldn't figure out was why I hadn't been shot at when I was comin' down from the cabin. Either that extra man had been part buried in the snow and just dug out, or he'd wanted to wait out Colleen. I needed to know more about where he was.

Slidin' loose the bonnet string on my hat, I took the hat off and took hold of the brim. I raised the hat just a bit above the edge of the log and moved it slowly. The lead went right through the hat.

But then there was a single shot from up at the cabin. It was the Winchester! Colleen! How could she have managed that rifle? But most important, had she hit the man? I had no way of knowin', not without settin' up some temptation for him. I moved my hat above the log again. But there was nothin'. I guess I couldn't figure he'd be dumb enough to bite twice runnin'. I gambled Colleen would have the rifleman covered if she hadn't hit him the first time, and the only way I could smoke him out was by takin' chances. I'd had my share that mornin'.

Doublin' my snowshoes up under me, I stood up and began to run across the flat. I dodged as best I could, runnin' from tree to tree, and I had my Colt ready in my hand. But there was no movement at all up where the shot had come from, and I wasn't drawin' fire.

I kept on going up that direction, and finally I located him. He was lyin' in the snow. That had to be the last of them, and I relaxed a little. I'd never seen the cowboy before. Colleen's shot had gone clean through his chest. I looked up toward the cabin and waved to Colleen, but I couldn't tell whether she was watchin' or not.

Holsterin' my Colt, I ran across the snow and climbed the ramp up to the cabin. Colleen was half sittin, half lyin' against the far wall. She was about unconscious. The kick from the Winchester had opened her shoulder again, and it was bleedin' bad. I got my snowshoes off, grabbed a handful of snow from the entrance and wrapped in the bloody neckerchief and put it to the wound. She smiled up at me and tried to sit up, but she was mighty weak.

Afterward, I wondered how Colleen ever made it down the mountain. I went to the corral and saddled up the horses, then came back up to the cabin, made coffee and heated some of the venison after I got the stove patched up some. Colleen seemed a little better, and she had some coffee, but she didn't seem up to eatin' much.

She indicated she was ready to go. By now her shoulder'd almost stopped bleedin', but it was an ugly mess. I cut a strip off one of the quilts and bound her arm as best I could to her body so it couldn't move and start the bleedin' again.

I'd decided to leave the Hoover horses, though I knew if a storm came up they'd likely starve before anyone could get back up there. But as we mounted Tempter and the pinto, Colleen motioned with her good arm for me to bring the horses with us, and we drive the Hoover string through the deep snow ahead of us, and started back down to town. It was after midnight when we finally made it onto the main street in Alta Vista.

Poor Doc, I knocked on his door and after a while he showed up.

"My God!" he said. "You made it!"

"Colleen's been shot, Doc. Help me get her off the horse. She'll be all right, I think, but she's so stiff from the shootin', I doubt she can move."

As we went out to the pinto, Doc asked, "Where's Hoover?"

"Those are their horses," I said, pointin' to the shadows that were movin' around the street. "All six of the men are dead!"

Doc looked across at me, and he never said a thing. When we got Colleen off the pinto and into his office, she smiled up at the both of us, and I knew she was goin' to be all right.

CHAPTER 18

By the time the snow had melted off Poncha six weeks later, Colleen had recovered most good as new. Her shoulder stayed a mite stiff, but she was back on her pinto right off, and there was no keepin' her back. Erla and Mike O'Malley hadn't let us forget about that second weddin', and we'd let the Hernandez family know we'd be comin'. I was busy cuttin' in my irrigation ditches, but I'd not forgotten the promise.

It was quite a procession as we rode on down through the San Luis valley. Erla and Mike drove their fancy rig. It was pulled by the most expensive team Mike could find in Denver. Ridin' alongside was Doc Train. Somehow he'd gotten that Morgan that Hoover used to have, and it suited Doc just right.

Comin' along, usually behind the rest of us, were Hans Mueller and Momma. Their children kept dartin' in and out like baby quails scootin' for cover. Some had their own ponies, some were on foot, and there even some young enough they made the whole trip ridin' on the wagon that was bein' pulled by a pair of heavy Percherons Mueller had insisted Mike buy for him just for the trip.

We all camped along the way, visited Saguache, then rode clear across the valley to the Circle R, and stayed overnight there. Slim Carruthers, he sat himself up on the fence outside the bunkhouse and told the Mueller brood tall stories about the frontier, stories which all seemed to have happened to him, but were really what he'd heard in barrooms from Santa Fe to Missoula.

When we left the Circle R for San Badillo, the Chalmers had joined us. The Mueller children were astonished when Jane Chalmers rode side saddle, 'cause they'd never seen anyone like that before. They tittered, dug their elbows into each other, and turned away in laughter when she spoke with her English accent.

Tina and Antonio had raced their ponies out to meet us north of San Badillo. The Mueller brood swarmed over them, and all the kids rode on ahead to tell Maria and Juan we were comin'.

Havin' been in San Badillo all the winter before, I'd got acquainted with Father Atencio, and I knew he ran his parish with a stern hand. Not that I could blame him if he was upset at bein' asked to conduct a wedding like ours, 'specially 'cause I knew he'd been told we were married five months before, by a nice German who had no church, and not even any papers that said he was a minister, and that we'd been livin' together ever since.

But I knew that on the frontier the Church was used to doin' some bendin' when it came to ceremonies. Father Atencio had only been in San Badillo less than two years, I knew that. But I figured it didn't take long bein' there 'til he could see that when Juan Hernandez asked a favor, it was a good thing to go along with it. I think Father Atencio understood that all right.

So we had the weddin' ceremony in the San Badillo parish church, and even if I was the one getting' married, I'd have to say it was a great wedding. Father Atencio did seem a mite mystified by it all, but he carried it off proper. He'd never married an Indian woman who couldn't say anything, but who obviously understood both English and Spanish, to a white man. But that wasn't all that surprised him, for he'd thought of Colleen as bein' Marguerita, the child of Maria and Juan Hernandez, but now of a sudden she seemed to have another mother and father, a giant man and his sweet faced wife, and they spoke no Spanish at all, and spoke English with an accent Father Atencio had never heard before. But what surprised him most, he told me afterward, was that Erla and Mike O'Malley spoke up right along with him when he came to the Latin parts of the weddin'.

About Hans Mueller and Momma, I don't think Father Atencio ever did really understand, and the best he hoped for was that their children would all sit quietly in the church during the weddin'. They did just fine.

Afterward, when we all came back to the Hernandez ranch, I watched Hans Mueller tryin' to discuss the Bible with Father Atencio. They had a hard go at it, but eventually both of them ended up with glasses in their hands, in front of the keg of Aguardiente. That was only a little part of the feast which Maria and Juan and the entire Hernandez clan had set up for us.

It looked to me the entire village was at the feast, and even by the time the sun came up the next mornin' there were still lots of folks enjoyin' themselves. Even Mike O'Malley, by that time, was tellin' me that Mexican weddin's were more fun than those his Irish kin had thought up.

It was late that afternoon when Doc Train hunted me up. Considerin' that our wedding had been mostly a time for fun, Doc was pretty serious when we sat down in the warm sun out on the Hernandez patio.

"Krieger," he began, "I need your advice. It's about the hospital here, and Senora Hernandez. Earlier this afternoon I spent two hours talking with her, and looking at what she intends to do here. You know, Krieger, she is a remarkable woman, and if your Ptarmigan mine is as profitable as I understand, she should be able to expand the hospital. Looking at the valley and at the patients she already has, the hospital is badly needed. Everything she knows about medicine she has taught herself. And Krieger, her fingers have the right touch. Your own wife would not be living if it were not for Maria Hernandez. Even you might not be alive.

"But what I wanted to ask is, would she let me volunteer to come down here a couple of times a year to help out? I think, also, I could get her some of the medical books she might need, maybe even written in Spanish."

Well, I couldn't see any reason not to talk it over with Maria, and when we did, she was excited. So it got arranged that Doc would come down the valley at least twice a year to help out with Maria's hospital.

The O'Malleys and the Muellers with their children, had already decided to drive on down to visit Santa Fe. Maria and Juan agreed to let Tina and Antonio go with them as interpreters. By the time they left, Doc Train had already started back to Alta Vista. I was anxious to get back home, and I'd promised we'd stop at the Circle R because Pete'd said he wanted to talk business with me.

When we got a chance to sit down in the living room, Pete started right out. "I just heard from the court in Denver, Krieger. The Circle R has been given all the cattle on the Hoover ranch because of the rustlin'. Whether they at first carried our brand or not, they now all belong to us. The land there is going to be sold. From what you've said, that ranch will never be worth a damn without the water you have. Hoover was a fool only when he bought the place. Afterwards, he was right in trying to talk Pollock into selling out to him.

"It took a little doin', but I found Irene Hoover in Denver. She's the one the land belongs to now. She's got no thought of coming back to Alta Vista. She hates the place, and she's anxious to sell. She knows we got the cattle, and she'll talk sense about the land.

"Krieger, if you know anything about Colorado, you just have to know that Alta Vista is going to be the center of a boom. I look for at least two railroads to come in there, and up in Denver they're even talkin' about a railroad that would go right up Sunshine Pass and across into Trevorton.

"Now, why don't you buy the land from Irene Hoover, the cattle from us, and go into the ranching business? It wouldn't make any sense for anyone else to have that land. If you want him, I'll let you have Slim Carruthers as foreman!"

Well, right off I could see that it all made sense. I couldn't put up any argument about that. The only trouble, I still didn't want to be a rancher. I just wanted to farm, and I knew there were plenty of differences. But the way Pete put it, I just couldn't pass up the chance to have the Hoover place, so we worked out the details right there, and I ended up buyin' the land from Irene Hoover, and the stock from Pete, and Slim Carruthers did come up as foreman.

By the end of summer, though, I knew I was wrong. I was spendin' more time on the irrigation at the farm and the crops I was tryin' to raise, than I was playin' nurse to a bunch of Hereford cows.

With Slim Carruthers, we were doin' all right, but my heart just wasn't in it. Colleen was spendin' more and more time up at the Hoover place, workin' with Slim.

She took to handlin' cattle just like a beaver takes to chewin' on aspen trees.

It was Slim Carruthers solved my problem. I'd not seen the answer, though it was right there in front of me all the time. The two of us had ridden across toward Squaw Gulch to look for some cows had wandered off, and Slim, he spoke up.

"Krieger," he said, "You'n me've been workin' together all summer, and I'd have to say you work hard. But you know, I've been around cows all my life, and I can size up a cowhand pretty quick. Krieger, you're a farmer, but you'll never be a rancher. You're more interested in that barley you're growin' down there, and how to get water to it, than any problem any cow is havin'. Don't get me wrong, I think I can run this string, and run it pretty well. But still, I need a boss, Krieger."

Well, I couldn't blame him for speakin' up, and I knew he was right. But Slim, he come up with an answer to the problem that surprised me.

"Best person we've had all summer helpin' run things is Colleen. She's just the finest cowhand I've ever seen, 'specially when she's on that cuttin' horse Mike

O'Malley gave her. Cattle take to her like no man I've knowed. It might sound funny comin' from me, Krieger, but that woman's a natural born ranch boss. Whyn't you turn the whole ranch over to her, and you get on with your irrigatin' and your crop raisin'?"

Well, that's the way it worked out. Carruthers was right. And Colleen and Slim Carruthers had a respect for each other that worked out just fine. There was some cowhands took exception to workin' for a woman, 'specially for an Indian. But that got itself settled pretty quick, Slim and I saw to that. And I expect maybe the stories that got told in the Mother Lode started some of those cowboys to thinkin' how Colleen might be a pretty interestin' boss to have, at that.

EPILOGUE

By the time the railroad was built to Alta Vista, and then up across Sunshine Pass, as Pete Chalmers had said might happen, Colorado'd become a state, and for the moment at least, Alta Vista was one of the important towns.

Passengers climbing down from the coaches that were stopped in the Alta Vista station often stared as they looked across the tracks and watched a beautiful, tall, straight backed woman astride a magnificent pinto horse. Like as not, she was riding bareback. But if she was on a saddle, they took note it was the most expensive saddle they'd ever seen.

Otto Mueller was the passenger agent by then, and he'd be standin' out there on the platform when the passengers got down.

"Who in hell's that?" someone was bound to ask.

"Oh," he'd reply quietly, but loud enough so everyone could hear, "That's Colleen Krieger. She runs the most famous ranch in Colorado, the K reverse K. Her husband, he's in the state legislature now, but he – him and my dad – they built most the irrigation systems in this whole valley. That's his farm you just passed by on the way across the flat. Was a time he was most famous for findin' gold, but now he's better known as a farmer – he likes farmin' better'n minin'. He and his wife used to own the Pollock Mine. The train'll stop up there just before it goes over the Pass. They made a lot of money when they sold out the mine, back a few years. He still owns part of the Ptarmigan Mine, that's down in San Badillo. Guess you've heard of that one..."

Then someone always asked, "But that woman's Indian, ain't she?"

"Sure is," Otto'd say. "A Ute, from down south of here. And before she became Colleen Krieger, she used to be known as Marguerita Hernandez, and then for a while before she got married she was Colleen O'Malley, and I went to her weddings, both of them. And I'll tell you, if she could talk, she could tell you more stories about the early days in the mountains than you could ever imagine."

"She can't talk?"

"Nope," he'd say. "An Apache lance cut through her throat when she was a baby. She's never said a word in her life."

Otto, he'd let that sink in a while, then he'd look at his watch, signal up to the engineer and say "Now, all aboard! We've got to get this train on up the Pass!"